The Oracle's Prophecy

Shadows of the Past, Keys to the Future

Victoria S. Grant

Copyright © 2024 by Victoria S. Grant.

All rights reserved. No part of this book may be used or reproduced in any form whatsoever without written permission except in the case of brief quotations in critical articles or reviews.

First Edition: April 2024

Table of Content

Chapter 1
The Artifact

In the vibrant heart of New York City, Nathanial Dove, a pragmatic private investigator, is distinguished by his rare talent for debunking archaeological forgeries. His office, a sanctuary amidst the chaos of urban life, is cluttered with relics of cases past—each artifact a testament to a mystery unraveled. Today, however, a call from the prestigious Manhattan Museum of Antiquity promises a challenge unlike any he has faced.

Nathanial, clad in his meticulously chosen attire that reflects both professionalism and a hint of skepticism, arrives at the museum. The building itself, an impressive structure of classical revival architecture, stands as a stark contrast to the glass-and-steel skyscrapers that surround it. He is greeted by Dr. Helen Carter, the museum's curator, whose enthusiasm about their newest acquisition—an ancient scroll believed to be from the Oracle of Delphi—is palpable and infectious, though Nathanial's demeanor remains guarded.

As they proceed to the secure examination room, Dr. Carter explains the scroll's origins and the mystery surrounding it. Nathanial listens, his skeptical mind cataloging every detail, preparing to unearth the truth beneath layers of historical sediment.

The scroll lies before him, encased in glass, its aged parchment whispering tales of ancient times. Nathanial begins his examination with a clinical precision that has become second nature. He inspects the material, the handwriting, the fading ink—his tools gliding from one test to another. Yet, his usual detachment waivers slightly under the scroll's enigmatic allure.

His discussion with Dr. Carter is peppered with technical jargon, explanations of forgery techniques, and anecdotes from his past cases, illustrating the depth of his expertise. This dialogue not only sets the foundation of his skeptical worldview but also highlights his openness to being proven wrong, a duality that makes him a uniquely compelling figure in his field.

As he delves deeper, Nathanial discovers a faintly etched pattern in the corner of the scroll. Driven by a mix of curiosity and the thrill of the hunt, he gently presses the pattern. A soft click breaks the silence, and suddenly, the scroll unfurls further, revealing hidden texts adorned with cryptic symbols and an ancient dialect of Greek.

Dr. Carter gasps, her excitement mirroring Nathanial's own accelerated pulse. Not because he believes in prophecies or mysticisms, but because he knows that this discovery, whether authentic or a clever forgery, could change the course of history.

The beat closes with Nathanial and Dr. Carter standing over the scroll, the morning light casting long shadows across the room. The museum outside remains a bubble of antiquity in the bustling city, but inside, a door to the past has been cracked open, beckoning Nathanial Dove into the shadows of history and myth. His journey into the mystical has unwittingly begun, guided by a document that challenges the very fabric of his beliefs.

The morning air was brisk as Nathanial Dove made his way through the bustling streets of Manhattan, his footsteps echoing with a firm resolve. The Manhattan Museum of Antiquity loomed ahead, its grand façade a silent sentinel in the heart of the city. As he approached, the contrast between the timeless architecture of the museum and the modern skyscrapers surrounding it was stark, underscoring the dual nature of his world—where the ancient and contemporary not only coexisted but often collided.

Inside, the museum was a cavernous space of marbled floors and high ceilings, where echoes of the past seemed to resonate against the walls.

Nathanial was met at the entrance by Dr. Helen Carter, whose reputation as a keen historian and curator preceded her. She greeted him with a warm, professional smile, extending a hand that Nathanial accepted with equal formality.

"Mr. Dove, it's a pleasure to finally meet you," Dr. Carter said, her voice a melodious contrast to the museum's solemn quietude. "I've followed your work for some time now. Your expertise will be invaluable today."

"Thank you, Dr. Carter," Nathanial replied, his tone polite yet reserved. "I'm intrigued by your new acquisition. Ancient scrolls are not typically part of my usual forgery cases."

As they walked towards the secure examination room, their conversation flowed from courteous introductions to the task at hand. The hallways were lined with artifacts that each told a silent story, and Nathanial felt the weight of history around him, pressing in with palpable intensity.

"The scroll was a part of a larger collection acquired from an estate sale in Greece," Dr. Carter explained as they entered a room that held the aura of both a library and a lab. "Its provenance is questionable, which is why your particular set of skills is essential."

Nathanial nodded, scanning the room filled with various analytical instruments and security measures designed to protect the museum's treasures. At the center of the room, the scroll awaited, encased in a glass cylinder that seemed to magnify its importance.

"Shall we?" Dr. Carter gestured towards the scroll.

"Certainly," Nathanial said, stepping closer. He pulled on a pair of gloves with practiced ease, the latex snapping slightly as they conformed to his hands. Dr. Carter observed his preparations, her curiosity clear.

"As you examine the scroll, I'd appreciate your thoughts on not just its authenticity, but also on any peculiarities you might notice," she said, her voice a mix of professional curiosity and a hint of something more—perhaps hope.

"Of course," Nathanial replied, his focus narrowing as he leaned in to inspect the artifact. His tools—a magnifier, a series of lights with varying intensity, and a small set of chemical reagents for preliminary testing—were laid out with meticulous care.

As he worked, Nathanial narrated his process, explaining his observations and the significance of each test. "The ink's age will tell us much about the scroll's authenticity. If it's a forgery, the forger might have used aged ink, but there are chemical signatures we can look for that are hard to fake."

Dr. Carter watched, fascinated. "I must admit, Mr. Dove, your reputation does not do you justice. Your method is quite thorough."

Nathanial offered a small, appreciative nod, too engrossed in his work to fully engage in modesty. "Thank you, Dr. Carter. In my line of work, the devil is often in the details."

The examination progressed, and as Nathanial continued his meticulous scrutiny, Dr. Carter's anticipation grew. The atmosphere in the room thickened with tension, a silent acknowledgment of the potential significance of their findings. They were on the brink of possibly rewriting a part of history or debunking a sophisticated fraud.

As the initial phase of the examination neared its end, Nathanial paused, his expression contemplative. "There's something unusual about the pattern of the ink dispersion," he remarked, adjusting his magnifier. "It suggests either a very skilled hand at forgery or genuine age. I'll need to conduct a few more tests to be certain."

Dr. Carter leaned in closer, her interest piqued. "I'm eager to hear your final thoughts, Mr. Dove."

Nathanial looked up, meeting her gaze with a mix of professionalism and the faintest trace of excitement. "Let's continue then, Dr. Carter. We may be standing on the precipice of a remarkable discovery."

Together, they turned back to the scroll, the promise of secrets yet unveiled hanging between them like the dust motes in the shafts of light streaming through the high windows. The museum, a vault of the past, held its breath as Nathanial Dove delved deeper into the mysteries it harbored.

In the hushed sanctity of the museum's examination room, the ancient scroll lay beneath the focused beams of specialized lighting equipment, its surface a map of intricate script and faded pigments. Nathanial, deeply engrossed in his task, adjusted his magnifier, scrutinizing each fiber of the parchment.

"See here, Dr. Carter," Nathanial pointed with a thin tool, careful not to touch the scroll itself. "The irregularities in the fiber suggest it's genuine papyrus. The patterning is consistent with known samples from the Hellenistic period."

Dr. Carter, standing adjacent with a notepad in hand, leaned closer. "Fascinating. And the ink? Could it have been replicated?"

"That's the next step." Nathanial selected a small device from his array of tools, a spectrometer, ready to test the ink's composition. "We're looking for anomalies in the elemental makeup that wouldn't be present in ancient inks."

As the device hummed softly, Nathanial continued, "Genuine ancient ink should primarily contain soot, binders, and maybe some organic materials—depending on the region and period."

"And if it's a forgery?" Dr. Carter asked, her pen poised above her notepad.

"We'd likely find modern synthetic pigments or anachronistic elements." The spectrometer beeped, and Nathanial checked the readout. "Hmm, this is good. No modern pigments. Everything so far is period-appropriate."

Dr. Carter jotted down notes, her excitement barely contained. "So, we might actually have a genuine artifact?"

"Possibly," Nathanial tempered the growing enthusiasm with caution. "Authenticating an artifact like this involves layers of verification. The material might be right, but we still need to verify the script and historical accuracy."

"Of course," Dr. Carter nodded, understanding the complexities involved. "What about the style of the script? Does it match the era?"

Nathanial switched to a digital microscope connected to a screen displaying the script in high resolution. "Let's analyze the calligraphy. Notice the form of the letters and the way the lines are executed. They should tell us if the scribe was trained in the styles prevalent at the time."

Dr. Carter watched the screen intently as Nathanial manipulated the controls, zooming in on specific characters. "These alpha and sigma forms are indeed typical of later Greek scripts, possibly even Alexandrian. The consistency of the stroke suggests a trained hand."

"This level of detail would be incredibly difficult for a forger to replicate accurately, wouldn't it?" Dr. Carter asked, her eyes not leaving the screen.

"Exactly. A forger might manage the general look, but these subtle nuances? It's unlikely. This is promising."

The examination moved to a deeper phase, with Nathanial delicately sampling a microscopic fragment of the ink for chemical analysis. "Now, we're checking for the binder. If we find animal glue, gum, or even egg— materials used in ancient times—we can be more confident about its authenticity."

Dr. Carter watched the process, her professional demeanor mixed with a hint of admiration for Nathanial's thoroughness. "Your meticulousness is quite impressive, Mr. Dove."

Nathanial offered a small smile, acknowledging the compliment. "Thank you, Dr. Carter. It's about respecting the artifact. Each piece has a story, and it's our job to listen."

The results from the chemical analysis slowly populated the screen, graphs, and numbers illustrating the molecular makeup. Nathanial interpreted the data with ease. "Look here, the binder. It's gum arabic, common in the region and period we suspected. This is looking more and more authentic."

Dr. Carter's excitement was palpable now. "So, we potentially have a real artifact from the Oracle of Delphi?"

"It seems so," Nathanial affirmed, his own voice tinged with excitement. "I'd be comfortable stating that the scroll is authentic, based on these findings. However, full authentication would also consider the historical context, which is where your expertise will be invaluable, Dr. Carter."

"Absolutely," Dr. Carter agreed enthusiastically. "I'll start correlating this with known historical texts and records from the Oracle. This could be a significant find, Nathanial."

As they wrapped up the examination, the weight of their discovery hung between them, a shared sense of purpose binding their efforts. Nathanial packed away his tools with the same precision he had unpacked them, his mind already racing ahead to the implications of their find.

Dr. Carter, equally thoughtful, watched him. "I'll prepare the necessary documentation and preliminary findings report. Nathanial, thank you for your expertise today."

"My pleasure, Dr. Carter. Keep me updated—I'm as eager as you are to see where this leads."

The scroll, now silent again in its glass case, seemed almost to glow under the museum lights, a beacon of ancient

----

As the examination continued, Nathanial's sharp eyes caught something unusual—a subtle, almost imperceptible discrepancy along the edge of the scroll. It was a faint pattern, differing slightly from the rest of the decorations that bordered the ancient manuscript.

"Dr. Carter, look at this," Nathanial called over, his voice low with a burgeoning curiosity. He adjusted the light to highlight the anomaly. "Do you see that? The pattern here is inconsistent with the rest."

Dr. Carter peered closely, her eyes narrowing in concentration. "Oh, you're right. It doesn't match the symmetrical consistency of the rest. Could it be damage, or...?"

"Or it's intentional," Nathanial interjected, his mind racing with possibilities. "This could be a deliberate feature. Maybe a kind of seal or... a trigger mechanism of some sort."

"A trigger? For what?" Dr. Carter's skepticism was evident, but her intrigue was piqued.

"Let's find out." With careful deliberation, Nathanial used a fine tool to gently probe the pattern. His hands were steady, his every move calculated under the watchful eye of Dr. Carter.

As he applied a slight pressure to the pattern, there was a soft but distinct click. Both of them froze, their breaths held in anticipation. Then, slowly, a section of the scroll began to unfurl that had previously resisted all attempts to be moved.

"It's moving," Dr. Carter whispered, her voice a mix of excitement and disbelief. "Nathanial, you were right. It's some kind of mechanical contrivance!"

As the hidden section of the scroll revealed itself, both leaned in closer. The new writings were different; they were in an ancient dialect, the symbols cryptic and compelling, suggesting a deeper, possibly mystical, significance.

"This is extraordinary," Dr. Carter breathed out, her eyes wide with wonder. "These could be additional prophecies—or perhaps something else entirely."

Nathanial nodded, equally transfixed. "This section looks older, or at least it's been protected from exposure. We need to document this immediately."

Dr. Carter quickly adjusted her notes, adding sketches of the newly revealed symbols. "Can you make anything out of this dialect? It doesn't look familiar."

Nathanial examined the text, his brow furrowed in concentration. "It's archaic, definitely pre-classical Greek, maybe even a form of Linear B script. We'll need a specialist in ancient languages to decipher this."

"Agreed. I'll arrange for that. For now, let's secure this section and ensure it's preserved properly," Dr. Carter said, her professional demeanor taking over once again.

Nathanial carefully stabilized the newly exposed section, ensuring that no further stress was placed on the ancient fibers. "We should also consider the possibility that this could be a hidden message, intended only for certain eyes. Its concealment suggests it was of great importance."

"That's a fascinating prospect," Dr. Carter mused, her mind already running through the implications. "A secret within a secret. This discovery could redefine our understanding of the Oracle's messages."

As they secured the scroll, their conversation turned to the logistics of what to do next. "I'll get in touch with the university. They have experts who can help us with the translation," Dr. Carter said, pulling out her phone to make calls.

"And I'll start compiling a detailed report on our findings so far," Nathanial added, his gaze lingering on the scroll. "Whatever is written here, it's been waiting a long time to be seen again."

The room fell quiet, save for the soft murmur of their movements and the occasional click of Dr. Carter's phone as she arranged for expert consultations. The weight of history was palpable in that quiet room, the silence speaking as loudly as their earlier conversation.

As Dr. Carter made her arrangements, Nathanial documented every detail of the scroll's new section, his hands steady and his mind awash with questions. What secrets did the ancient text hold? And what consequences might their unveiling bring?

The late afternoon sun cast long shadows across the room, stretching over the floor and up the walls, as if trying to reach into the past that Nathanial and Dr. Carter were slowly unraveling.

Chapter 2
The Hidden Mechanism

In the dimly lit confines of the museum's specialized laboratory, the atmosphere was thick with anticipation. Nathanial and Dr. Helen Carter stood side by side over the scroll, which lay partially unfurled on the examination table, its newly discovered contents illuminated under a gentle, precise light. Dr. Emily Stanton, a renowned linguist known for her expertise in ancient dialects, had just joined them, her presence signaling the start of a deeper exploration into the scroll's secrets.

"Thank you for coming on such short notice, Dr. Stanton," Nathanial greeted, his voice tinged with both gratitude and urgency.

"It's not every day you get a call about a new discovery from the Oracle of Delphi," Dr. Stanton replied, her eyes already fixated on the scroll. "Let's see what has remained hidden all these centuries."

Dr. Carter handed her a magnifier. "We believe this section might be in Linear B script, or something closely related. It's entirely unlike the main text."

Dr. Stanton leaned in, her expert eyes scanning the ancient symbols. "Yes, I see why you called me. This is indeed a rare form of Linear B, used primarily for sacred or highly secretive communications. This could be a significant find."

Nathanial watched her work, his curiosity mounting with each passing moment. "Can you make anything out yet?"

"Give me a few moments," Dr. Stanton murmured, her focus absolute. After a brief pause, her expression shifted, a mix of awe and excitement molding her features. "Yes, I can read parts of it. It's fragmentary, but there's mention of a 'pathway' and 'hidden knowledge'. There are also references to specific rituals and astronomical alignments."

"Astronomical alignments?" Dr. Carter leaned closer, her interest piqued. "Could this be related to the prophecy's predictions of calamities, or perhaps something else?"

"It's too early to say for certain," Dr. Stanton cautioned, "but this seems more instructional than prophetic. It's like a guide."

Nathanial considered this. "A guide for what, exactly? And why go to such lengths to hide this part of the scroll?"

"That will require more translation and context," Dr. Stanton replied. "But it's clear that whoever concealed this information deemed it extremely important, possibly dangerous."

"Dangerous in what way?" Dr. Carter asked, a note of concern threading through her voice.

"Knowledge, especially of the sacred and secret variety, can be powerful and perilous," Dr. Stanton explained. "If it pertains to rituals that could manipulate events or perceptions, it would have been guarded closely."

Nathanial nodded thoughtfully. "We need to fully understand what this text is telling us. Any knowledge that could potentially manipulate historical or natural events would indeed be dangerous in the wrong hands."

Dr. Carter looked between Nathanial and Dr. Stanton, her resolve firming. "Then our next step is clear. We need a full translation, and we need to understand the historical and cultural context surrounding these references to rituals and alignments."

"I'll need to take high-resolution images and work with them on my systems back at the university," Dr. Stanton suggested. "I can apply some digital enhancements to clarify the text."

"Whatever you need, we'll support you," Dr. Carter assured her, determination evident in her stance. "This could change our understanding of the ancient world."

As Dr. Stanton prepared to transport the necessary images and data she needed for her translation work, Nathanial documented every detail of their current findings. The air in the lab was charged with a palpable sense of discovery, tinged with the tension of the unknown.

Once Dr. Stanton had everything she needed, she paused, looking back at the scroll with a speculative glint in her eye. "We might be on the brink of uncovering something truly monumental."

Nathanial and Dr. Carter exchanged a look, their shared excitement a silent bond between them. "Keep us updated, Emily. The sooner we understand, the sooner we can decide our next steps."

With Dr. Stanton's departure, the room felt suddenly quiet, the weight of history pressing down upon Nathanial and Dr. Carter. They stood together, contemplating the scroll and its secrets, aware that the path they were about to walk could alter their understanding of the past in unforeseen ways.

The museum's conference room had been converted into a temporary research hub. Nathanial Dove and Dr. Helen Carter sat at a large oval table, surrounded by books, ancient manuscripts, and digital displays. Across from them, Dr. Emily Stanton, the linguist, was joined by Dr. Richard Ames, a historian specializing in ancient Greek civilizations, and Dr. Laura Zheng, an astronomer whose expertise in historical celestial events was unparalleled. The atmosphere was thick with anticipation, the air crackling with the energy of impending revelations.

"Thank you all for joining this consultation," Dr. Carter began, her voice steady, betraying none of her underlying excitement. "We've uncovered a section of the scroll that appears to be quite significant, potentially altering our understanding of certain ancient Greek practices."

Dr. Stanton nodded, ready with her tablet displaying enhanced images of the scroll. "I've made some progress on the translation. The text mentions a 'pathway' that seems to be both literal and metaphorical, possibly a pilgrimage or a ritual processional route linked to celestial events."

Dr. Ames leaned forward, intrigued. "That's consistent with some practices we know were associated with major temples and oracles. These pathways were not just physical journeys but spiritual quests, often aligning with stars or significant astrological configurations."

Dr. Zheng chimed in, tapping on her laptop to bring up a star map. "If we can identify the celestial alignments mentioned, we might be able to pinpoint the exact timing or significance of these events. It could tell us more about the 'when' of these rituals."

Nathanial, ever the pragmatist, interjected, "But how can we be sure the text refers to actual stars and not metaphorical ones? The ancients often used celestial imagery in their religious texts without it corresponding to observable astronomical phenomena."

"That's a valid point," Dr. Zheng acknowledged, adjusting her glasses. "However, if we cross-reference the dates and descriptions with known astronomical records from the period, we might find overlapping data that supports a literal interpretation."

Dr. Stanton scrolled through her translations. "There's mention of a 'darkened sun' and a 'hidden moon,' which I interpreted as possible references to eclipses. These could serve as markers for timing these rituals."

"An eclipse would certainly be significant enough to warrant encoding its details in such a secretive manner," Dr. Ames added. "Eclipses were often seen as omens or divine messages."

Dr. Carter took meticulous notes as the discussion unfolded. "Emily, can you determine any specific dates from the text, or do we need more context?"

"I'll need to dive deeper into the syntax and phrasing used," Dr. Stanton replied. "The language is dense and symbolic. But with Richard's historical context and Laura's astronomical data, we might piece together a timeline."

Nathanial looked around at the group, their faces illuminated by the glow of their screens, a testament to the convergence of ancient lore and modern technology. "Let's prioritize identifying any potential dates and locations. If this text is guiding us towards a specific time and place, understanding that could be key to unlocking its full meaning."

Dr. Zheng nodded, already pulling up software to simulate ancient sky maps. "I'll start with a broad analysis of celestial events around the presumed date range of the scroll. We'll look for any eclipses that might correspond with Emily's translations."

"And I'll review historical accounts of rituals and events from the surrounding regions during those times," Dr. Ames offered. "We need to ensure the historical accuracy of any hypotheses we develop."

Dr. Stanton looked between her colleagues, her expression resolute. "And I'll continue refining the translation, focusing on any terms that could be astronomically relevant. We need to understand exactly what the ancients believed they were doing."

As the meeting drew to a close, the team set their plan into motion, each expert diving into their respective realms of knowledge. The room buzzed with the sound of tapping keys and whispered theories, a symphony of scholarship that bridged millennia.

Dr. Carter watched the team with a sense of pride and wonder, her thoughts drifting to the possibilities that lay hidden within the ancient text. What secrets did the ancients encode in the scroll, and what truths awaited their discovery? As the experts worked, the pieces of a long-forgotten puzzle began to click into place, hinting at revelations that might soon illuminate the shadows of history.

Back in his office at the museum, Nathanial Dove sat surrounded by the echoes of ancient mysteries, the scroll's revelations sprawled out before him on digital screens and printouts. Dr. Helen Carter joined him, bringing fresh insights from the team's latest research meeting.

"Nathanial, the team's making progress, but I sense you're still holding onto some reservations," Dr. Carter observed, placing a stack of notes on the desk. Her intuition about Nathanial's skepticism was as sharp as ever.

Nathanial leaned back in his chair, crossing his arms thoughtfully. "I am, Helen. It's not the authenticity of the scroll that concerns me—it's the interpretations we're putting forward. History is rife with examples where significant misreadings have led scholars down erroneous paths."

Dr. Carter nodded, understanding his caution. "That's a fair point. However, the alignments Dr. Zheng has found in the celestial records are compelling. She matched several references in the scroll with historical astronomical events."

"True, but correlation isn't causation," Nathanial countered, tapping a pen against his notepad. "Just because events in the sky coincide with what's written doesn't necessarily mean the ancients interpreted them the way we're assuming."

Dr. Carter sighed, conceding the point. "Let's review what we know. Dr. Stanton has confirmed that the language used in the hidden section is not just archaic but ceremonial. It suggests a purpose beyond mere record-keeping—something intended for a specific, perhaps elite, audience."

"And that's another thing," Nathanial interjected. "If this was meant for a select few, how broad could its impact really have been? Are we inflating the importance of a text that might have been obscure even in its own time?"

Dr. Carter considered this, her fingers drumming lightly on the table. "It's possible. But consider the effort made to hide this section. Why go through such lengths if it wasn't of significant value?"

Nathanial paused, the historian in him wrestling with the detective. "Alright, let's hypothesize it was important. The question then becomes, what exactly were they trying to achieve with this 'pathway' and these rituals? And how might it relate to the broader societal or cultural constructs of the time?"

"That's what we need to pinpoint," Dr. Carter agreed. "Richard is delving into the socio-political climates around the supposed dates. He's looking for any major events that might align with our findings—wars, famines, leadership changes. Anything that could provide context."

"And Laura's work on the celestial alignments?" Nathanial asked, his curiosity piqued despite his skepticism.

"She's refining her models based on Emily's translations. They're focusing on eclipses because of their symbolic and physical visibility. People of that era would have seen them as powerful omens."

Nathanial nodded slowly, his analytical mind processing the influx of information. "I suppose if we can anchor our translations to specific, historically documented events, it would lend more weight to our interpretations."

"Exactly," Dr. Carter said, her voice firm with determination. "And while your skepticism is valuable—it keeps us rigorous—we should also embrace the intrigue of what we might uncover."

Nathanial smiled, appreciating her perspective. "Intrigue indeed. It's what pulled me into this field in the first place. Let's keep pushing forward, Helen. Where do we stand with the next steps?"

Dr. Carter pulled up her digital planner, outlining the schedule. "Emily will have another set of translations ready by tomorrow. She and Laura are coordinating to match those texts with specific dates. Meanwhile, Richard's exploring the historical archives for any anomalies during those times."

"Good," Nathanial replied, his mind already racing ahead. "Keep me updated on their findings. And Helen, make sure they know to double-check their assumptions at every step. We're treading on groundbreaking territory here."

As Dr. Carter left to relay the instructions, Nathanial turned his attention back to the myriad of documents before him. Each piece of parchment, each digital byte of ancient wisdom, was a puzzle piece in a much larger picture that was slowly coming into focus. The thrill of the chase, the allure of unveiling history's secrets, rekindled his passion, intertwining with his skepticism to forge a path forward in unraveling the mysteries of the ancient scroll.

As the day drew to a close and the shadows lengthened across his cluttered office, Nathanial Dove was still poring over the latest communications from his team of experts. The air was heavy with the musky scent of old books and the modern buzz of computer screens displaying ancient constellations. The ring of his phone cut sharply through the quiet concentration, an unexpected interruption that Nathanial viewed with a slight frown.

Picking up the receiver, Nathanial's voice was calm but edged with fatigue. "Nathanial Dove."

The voice that answered was distorted, a deliberate modulation that sent a chill down Nathanial's spine despite his usual composure. "Mr. Dove, you're treading on dangerous ground. Be careful not to dig too deep."

Nathanial straightened, his weariness replaced by alertness. "Who is this? What are you talking about?"

But the line went dead, leaving only a soft click and the hum of the dial tone. Nathanial sat back, the phone still in his hand, his mind racing through possible implications of the cryptic warning.

Moments later, Dr. Helen Carter knocked and entered his office, her face alight with the excitement of their discoveries. She stopped short upon seeing Nathanial's troubled expression. "Is everything alright, Nathanial?"

Nathanial placed the phone down, his gaze distant. "I just received a mysterious warning. Someone doesn't want us pursuing this any further."

Dr. Carter's excitement faded, replaced by concern. "A warning? From whom?"

"I don't know. The voice was disguised. But the message was clear—stop our investigation."

Dr. Carter sat down opposite him, her brow furrowed in thought. "Do you think it's credible? We've been very careful about security."

Nathanial leaned forward, his eyes narrowing. "It's hard to say. But it suggests we're onto something significant. Maybe even more significant than we realized."

"Do you think it's related to the scroll's contents? Perhaps there's more at stake here than historical knowledge," Dr. Carter mused, tapping her fingers on the desk.

"That's my concern," Nathanial admitted. "This scroll, if it indeed holds the power to influence or predict, could be valuable to many, not just historians or academics."

Dr. Carter nodded slowly. "What do you propose we do?"

"We need to increase our security, for starters. And perhaps it's time to involve someone from outside—someone who can provide a different kind of protection," Nathanial suggested, his mind already sorting through possible contacts in security and law enforcement.

"I agree. I'll start by enhancing our digital security, make sure all our communications are encrypted," Dr. Carter said, her voice determined. "I'll also review who has access to our findings."

Nathanial stood, his decision firm. "And I'll reach out to an old colleague from my law enforcement days. If there are threats, we should be prepared."

Dr. Carter rose too, her stance resolute. "Let me know how I can assist. We can't let this warning stop us, Nathanial. What we've discovered could change our understanding of history."

Nathanial managed a small smile, appreciating her steadfastness. "We won't back down, Helen. Let's proceed cautiously but with resolve. We have to see this through, no matter what shadows we may find ourselves up against."

As Dr. Carter left to implement the new security measures, Nathanial turned back to his work, his eyes lingering on the images of the scroll. The mystery of the ancient text was deepening, the stakes growing ever higher as they delved into the shadows of the past. The evening stretched out before him, filled with the glow of his computer screens and the weight of the unknown. Whatever lay ahead, Nathanial Dove was ready to face it, fortified by curiosity and a newfound caution.

Chapter 3
The Prophecy Unfolds

Late one evening in his office, with the glow of the city lights casting shadows through the blinds, Nathanial Dove sat across from Dr. Emily Stanton. They were surrounded by layers of ancient texts, digital screens flickering with celestial maps, and a palpable sense of unease that had settled over the room since the mysterious warning.

Nathanial rubbed his temples, feeling the weight of their discoveries. "Emily, the alignments you and Laura have pinpointed—are they as unsettling as I think they are?"

Dr. Stanton, her face illuminated by the soft light of her laptop, nodded gravely. "Indeed, they are. The celestial events we've mapped out align too closely with the dates and descriptions in the scroll. It's almost as if whoever wrote this had foreknowledge of these events."

Nathanial leaned forward, his interest piqued despite the tension. "Foreknowledge, or was it something more deliberate? Could they have been using this as a guide to plan or predict?"

"That's one theory," Dr. Stanton replied, scrolling through her notes. "The text doesn't just align with natural events; it aligns with major socio-political upheavals as well. It's as if the text served as a blueprint for influencing or anticipating significant shifts."

"Could this be why someone warned us off?" Nathanial mused, connecting dots as he spoke. "If there's power in this knowledge—"

"—Then it's power that someone might still want to wield, or keep hidden," Dr. Stanton finished his thought, her tone somber.

The door to Nathanial's office opened, and Dr. Helen Carter stepped in, her expression tense. "I just got off the phone with Richard. He's found references in the historical archives that might explain some of the social upheavals mentioned in the scroll. It seems these events were not only predicted but perhaps orchestrated."

Nathanial exchanged a look with Dr. Stanton. "Orchestrated? You mean, someone could have used the knowledge of the scrolls to manipulate events? To what end?"

"That's what we need to find out," Dr. Carter said, setting down a stack of historical journals on the desk. "If we can understand the motives and methods, perhaps we can understand why this knowledge was so guarded—and why it's still dangerous."

Dr. Stanton adjusted her glasses, her gaze fixed on the screens displaying the celestial alignments. "This goes beyond academic curiosity now. We're dealing with something that could be very current and very real."

Nathanial stood, pacing the room slowly as he thought. "We need to tread carefully. Whoever warned me might not be the only one watching our progress."

"I've increased security around our digital communications and our physical access to the archives and labs," Dr. Carter assured him, but her voice carried an edge of worry.

"We should consider bringing in security consultation," Nathanial suggested, stopping to look at both women. "If our research is putting us in danger, we need to be proactive."

Dr. Stanton closed her laptop, her face set in a determined line. "Agreed. But let's not lose momentum. I'll coordinate with Laura to refine our celestial data. The more precise we are, the better we can understand the timelines."

"And I'll dig deeper into the historical context with Richard," Dr. Carter added, picking up one of the journals. "There might be more hidden in the annals of history that we've overlooked."

Nathanial nodded, his resolve firming. "And I'll start reaching out to some security professionals. If our findings are as potent as we fear, we need to ensure they're protected—along with ourselves."

As Dr. Stanton and Dr. Carter prepared to leave, Nathanial turned back to his desk, his eyes lingering on the illuminated manuscripts and digital displays. The night outside was deep and quiet, but the work within his office burned bright, casting light on shadows long left untouched. Whatever secrets the ancient scroll held, Nathanial Dove was determined to uncover them, shielded by caution but driven by an unquenchable thirst for the truth.

Early the next morning, Nathanial Dove was jolted from his analysis by an urgent call from Dr. Laura Zheng, the astronomer collaborating closely on the project. Her voice was laced with a mix of excitement and apprehension, a combination that Nathanial had become all too familiar with during their investigation.

"Nathanial, you need to see this," Dr. Zheng insisted, her words tumbling out rapidly. "One of the celestial events we identified from the scroll—it's happening. There's a solar eclipse occurring much sooner than expected, aligning perfectly with our calculations."

Nathanial's pulse quickened. "Are you certain? This could be the first real test of the scroll's accuracy."

"Absolutely," Dr. Zheng affirmed. "I've triple-checked the data. The alignment is unmistakable. And there's more—you know the associated predictions of upheaval? We might be seeing the beginnings of that as well."

Nathanial leaned forward, his mind racing. "What's happening?"

"There have been sudden, unexplained power outages across the city starting just minutes ago," Dr. Zheng reported. "It could be a coincidence, but given the timing with the eclipse, it's... unsettling."

"This is exactly the kind of sign we've been warned could follow," Nathanial said, his voice grave. He paused, considering the implications. "I'm heading to your lab. We need to monitor this closely."

Minutes later, Nathanial arrived at the observatory where Dr. Zheng and her team were tracking the celestial events. Screens displaying real-time data filled the room with a soft, electronic glow. Dr. Zheng pointed to a live feed of the eclipse on a large monitor, the moon slowly obscuring the sun in a dark silhouette against the bright sky.

"As fascinating as this is, the potential real-world effects are what concern me," Nathanial remarked, his gaze fixed on the screens.

"Indeed," Dr. Zheng replied, switching to a data visualization showing the city's power grid. "Look at this—the outages began in the east and are spreading. If this pattern continues, it could match the 'shadow path' described in the scroll."

Nathanial's concern deepened. "We need to alert the authorities, give them a heads-up in case this escalates."

"I'll handle that," Dr. Zheng said, reaching for her phone. "In the meantime, can you contact Dr. Carter and Dr. Stanton? They should be aware that what we considered theoretical is manifesting."

Nathanial nodded, quickly dialing Dr. Carter. When she answered, her voice was anxious, already aware of the unfolding events. "Nathanial, I've seen the news. The power outages—they're exactly where the eclipse's shadow is falling, aren't they?"

"Yes, and it's no random occurrence," Nathanial confirmed. "It lines up too closely with the prophecy. This might be the first sign, Helen. The first proof that there's truth to what's written."

Dr. Carter was silent for a moment, absorbing the gravity of the situation. "What do you suggest we do?"

"We stay the course," Nathanial replied firmly. "Keep digging, keep analyzing. But let's also prepare for other possible signs. This could be just the beginning."

"Agreed," Dr. Carter said. "I'll loop in Emily and Richard. We need to understand if there are more events predicted that we should be watching for."

After hanging up, Nathanial turned back to the screens, his eyes tracing the creeping shadow of the eclipse across the digital maps. The room was filled with a tense anticipation, every scientist and technician on edge as they watched the phenomenon unfold.

As the darkness of the eclipse reached its peak, the room dimmed, plunged into an eerie twilight that seemed to echo the darkening sky outside. Nathanial stood beside Dr. Zheng, both of them silent witnesses to a historical alignment that was proving to be more than just an astronomical curiosity.

Their work, driven by the deciphered secrets of an ancient scroll, was no longer confined to theoretical debates or historical analysis. It was becoming a tangible, impactful reality, and as the light slowly began to return, both the sun and the truth seemed to emerge together from behind the shadow.

As the solar eclipse receded, leaving behind a trail of unexplained power outages and a city buzzing with both confusion and awe, Nathanial Dove felt a growing resolve. The day's events had been too aligned with the prophecies and too significant to dismiss as mere coincidences. The impact of what they had uncovered was becoming impossible to ignore.

In the aftermath, Nathanial convened a late-night meeting in the observatory's main conference room, the walls lined with celestial maps and ancient astrological charts. The air was thick with the scent of coffee and the undercurrent of urgency. Dr. Helen Carter, Dr. Emily Stanton, and Dr. Laura Zheng were gathered around the table, each displaying varying degrees of concern and excitement.

"We've seen today what might just be the beginning of what the scroll predicted," Nathanial began, his voice steady despite the weight of his words. "The eclipse and the outages aren't just isolated events—they're possibly the first tangible signs that the prophecies are more than just ancient myths."

Dr. Zheng, still poring over data from the day's celestial event, nodded in agreement. "The alignment was precise, unnervingly so. And the subsequent outages followed the path of the eclipse across the city exactly as the shadow passed."

Dr. Stanton added, "The text was clear about a 'darkening' followed by 'chaos below,' which we assumed was metaphorical. Maybe it was literal."

Dr. Carter interjected, "If we accept that these events are connected to the prophecies, we need to understand the full scope of what might be coming. The other events described in the scroll—do we have estimates on when they might occur?"

"That's what we need to figure out next," Nathanial replied. "Laura, can your team continue to monitor celestial events and align them with the scroll's timeline?"

"We're already on it," Dr. Zheng confirmed. "We'll need to keep a close watch on any anomalies in both celestial patterns and earthly phenomena."

Nathanial turned his attention to Dr. Stanton. "Emily, how much more of the scroll's text can we decipher quickly? We need to know what to watch for."

"I'll prioritize sections that reference specific signs or events. It's fragmentary, but with focused effort, we should be able to piece together more of the puzzle," Dr. Stanton assured him.

"And I will review historical records again," Dr. Carter added. "There might be past incidents that were influenced by similar alignments. We could learn from those."

As the meeting drew to a close, Nathanial felt the weight of their task. They were not just researchers anymore; they were sentinels, watching for signs of ancient predictions unfolding in real time. The group dispersed, each to their respective tasks, with a new sense of purpose.

Nathanial stayed behind, his eyes scanning over the scroll's images and translations spread across the table. The quiet of the room was a stark contrast to the turmoil of the day, providing him with a moment to reflect on the path they were on. The discoveries had not only illuminated aspects of the ancient world but were also shedding light on how deeply interconnected celestial and terrestrial events could be.

As he organized his notes and planned his next steps, Nathanial felt a surge of determination. The challenges ahead were daunting, but the pursuit of understanding—of truth—was a powerful motivator. He knew that whatever the scroll held, whatever secrets were yet to be uncovered, they were significant not just to history, but to the very fabric of the present.

With a final glance at the data screens still flickering with the day's analyses, Nathanial turned off the lights and stepped out into the night. The city around him was calm now, the earlier chaos subdued, but the echoes of the day's revelations lingered, a reminder of the delicate balance between light and darkness, knowledge and mystery.

In the days following the unsettling eclipse and citywide disturbances, Nathanial Dove intensified his preparations, recognizing that they might be on the cusp of further manifestations of the ancient prophecies. The scroll's cryptic messages were no longer mere artifacts of history; they had become harbingers of potential realities that demanded respect and readiness.

In his office, cluttered with papers and ancient texts, Nathanial met with Dr. Helen Carter and Dr. Emily Stanton to strategize their next steps. Maps of celestial patterns were spread out on the table, alongside timelines of predicted events.

"We need to be proactive," Nathanial stated firmly, looking from one expert to the other. "It's not just about interpreting the scroll anymore. It's about anticipating what might happen next."

Dr. Carter nodded, her expression serious. "The historical parallels we've found suggest that the next event could occur within the month. The references to 'water rising' could imply a flood or storm. We should monitor weather patterns closely."

Dr. Stanton, who had been translating more of the scroll, chimed in, "The latest translations mention 'the earth trembling.' We might also be looking at seismic activity. I recommend we consult with a geologist."

"That's a good idea," Nathanial agreed. "Let's bring in Dr. Allen; his expertise in seismic anomalies will be invaluable."

As the team discussed logistical preparations, Nathanial's phone buzzed with an alert from Dr. Laura Zheng. He excused himself to take the call, stepping aside for privacy.

"Laura, what's the update?" Nathanial asked, his tone urgent.

"We've noticed an unusual pattern in the tidal forces," Dr. Zheng reported. "It's subtle, but it aligns with some of the celestial configurations we've been tracking. This could be what the scroll referred to as 'the moon's pull increasing.'"

"Keep monitoring it, and send me updates every hour," Nathanial instructed. "I'll relay this to the team. We might need to start looking at coastal areas for any unusual activity."

Returning to the table, Nathanial relayed the new information. "Laura's observed anomalies in tidal forces. We might be dealing with more than just theoretical threats. This could get real, very quickly."

Dr. Carter was already on her laptop, pulling up additional data. "I'll cross-reference historical flood events with celestial alignments. Maybe we can narrow down potential locations and timings."

As the meeting progressed, the atmosphere was thick with a mix of intellectual excitement and the weight of responsibility. Each revelation from the scroll brought with it a need for immediate action, turning the team into a makeshift rapid response unit, albeit one grounded in historical and astronomical analysis.

After the meeting, Nathanial lingered in the room, reviewing notes and preparing for the possibility of traveling to potentially affected areas. The thought of witnessing prophecy unfold was both exhilarating and daunting.

That night, Nathanial experienced a vivid dream. He stood by the ocean, watching as the calm sea began to churn violently under a starlit sky. The dream felt prophetic, a premonition perhaps, reflecting the anxiety and anticipation of their recent findings.

The next morning, Nathanial shared his experience with Dr. Carter, who listened intently. "Your subconscious is clearly processing all we've uncovered," she said thoughtfully. "But it might also be a sign. We should consider all possibilities, no matter how unscientific they might seem."

Nathanial nodded, his usual skepticism softened by the events of the past few days. "I agree. Let's keep our minds open to all interpretations. The ancients believed in the power of omens. Maybe we should too, at least for now."

As they resumed their work, the team was more united and driven than ever, their collective efforts a blend of science, history, and a touch of the mystical. They were no longer just researchers; they were sentinels at the gates of potential futures, guided by the cryptic warnings of a long-silent oracle. Their preparations continued, deep into the realm of both known science and speculative prophecy, ready for whatever the ancient texts might predict next.

Chapter 4
Journey to Greece

Nathanial Dove and Dr. Helen Carter stepped off the plane into the bustling Athens International Airport, greeted by the warm Mediterranean sun and the distant view of the city's historic skyline. Their arrival in Greece was marked not only by a sense of urgency but also an undercurrent of excitement about the potential discoveries awaiting them in this ancient land.

"Here we are, Helen," Nathanial remarked as they navigated through the busy terminal. "Athens. It feels like stepping right into history."

"It does," Dr. Carter agreed, adjusting her bag on her shoulder. "I've arranged for us to meet with Professor Nikos Demetriou at the National Archaeological Museum first thing tomorrow. He's expecting us and has agreed to help with our investigation."

"That's excellent," Nathanial replied. "His expertise on ancient Greek rituals and their celestial connections could be invaluable. Do you think he'll have insights into the specific locations mentioned in the scroll?"

"I'm hopeful," Dr. Carter said as they made their way to the baggage claim. "He's one of the leading experts on oracular sites. If anyone can help us pinpoint the locations, it's him."

As they collected their luggage, Nathanial's phone buzzed with a message from Dr. Laura Zheng. He quickly read the update on the latest celestial observations related to their project.

"Laura's team has just sent through the latest data," Nathanial informed Dr. Carter. "They've confirmed another alignment event is due in just a few days. It seems our timing couldn't be more critical."

Dr. Carter's expression grew serious. "Let's hope we find what we need quickly then. The sooner we understand the connections between these sites and the celestial events, the better we can prepare for what might happen."

Exiting the airport, they hailed a taxi to take them to their hotel in the heart of Athens. The drive offered them views of the city's blend of ancient and modern architecture, a vivid reminder of the layers of history they were about to delve into.

"Once we're settled," Nathanial started, outlining their plan, "we should go over the scroll translations again. I want to make sure we're absolutely clear on what we're looking for when we visit these sites."

"Agreed," Dr. Carter nodded. "I'll also compile all the historical data we have related to the periods in question. The more context we have, the better."

The taxi wound its way through the bustling streets, passing landmarks and everyday scenes of city life until they reached their hotel. After checking in and taking a moment to refresh, they regrouped in the hotel lobby, maps and documents spread out before them.

"Here's the list of sites we need to visit," Dr. Carter said, pointing out locations on a map. "Based on Emily's translations, these are the most likely to correspond with the events described in the scroll."

Nathanial studied the map closely. "We'll start with the Temple of Olympian Zeus. It's nearby, and its historical significance could be a key factor in understanding the larger puzzle."

Dr. Carter looked thoughtful. "Yes, and I've read about underground chambers there that were only recently discovered. They might not be open to the public, but I'm sure Professor Demetriou could help us gain access."

"Perfect," Nathanial said with a nod. "Tomorrow's meeting with him can't come soon enough."

As they gathered their materials, ready to retire for the evening after a long day of travel, the historical weight of their surroundings seemed to press upon them. Each step they took was a step further into a mystery centuries in the making, each discovery a piece of a larger, more complex puzzle that connected the distant past with the urgent present.

"Let's get a good night's rest," Nathanial suggested as they headed towards the elevator. "We'll need all our energy for tomorrow."

Dr. Carter agreed, her mind already on the day ahead. "Indeed, Nathanial. We're not just chasing shadows of the past; we're racing against time."

With that, they ascended to their rooms, the city of Athens sprawling out beneath them, ancient and enduring, holding its secrets close until they could uncover them under the light of both sun and stars.

In the cool, shadow-filled halls of the National Archaeological Museum of Athens, Nathanial Dove and Dr. Helen Carter met with Professor Nikos Demetriou, a distinguished historian with a deep knowledge of ancient Greek oracular sites. They gathered around a table laden with artifacts and parchment scrolls, the air thick with the musty scent of antiquity.

"Professor Demetriou, thank you for meeting with us," Dr. Carter began, extending a hand in greeting. "We are here to gain a deeper understanding of some specific sites mentioned in an ancient scroll we are studying."

"Of course," the professor responded warmly, gesturing towards the documents and items on the table. "I am intrigued by your project. Tell me more about these sites and how they connect to your scroll."

Nathanial took the lead, unfolding a replica of the scroll on the table. "Our findings suggest that certain celestial events mentioned in this scroll align with historical and possibly ritualistic events at these sites." He pointed to marked locations on a map of ancient Greece.

"Interesting," Professor Demetriou murmured, adjusting his glasses and leaning in to examine the script. "These symbols here correspond to divine interactions—common in oracular pronouncements. Which sites are you focusing on?"

"We are particularly interested in the Temple of Olympian Zeus and the Sanctuary of Delphi," Dr. Carter answered, pointing to the detailed notes they had compiled.

"Ah, both are pivotal in understanding the religious and astronomical practices of the ancient Greeks," the professor noted. "The Temple of Olympian Zeus was not just a place of worship but also a location where celestial alignments were observed. Its architecture aligns with specific solar events."

Nathanial's interest peaked. "And what of Delphi? Our scroll hints at a hidden chamber or pathway linked to the Oracle."

"Delphi is, of course, central to Greek mysticism and prophecy," Professor Demetriou explained. "There are lesser-known underground sections of the complex, some only recently explored, that suggest it was a site of significant celestial and mystical importance, possibly even containing hidden rooms or artifacts meant to enhance the Oracle's connection to the divine."

Dr. Carter quickly jotted down notes. "Could these places have been part of a larger network or design linked to the prophecies we're studying?"

"It's highly plausible," the professor continued. "Many ancient sites were interconnected not just physically but also through shared celestial and religious significance. They could have been part of a vast sacred geography, each part contributing to a whole, a kind of ancient wisdom map."

"This aligns with some of our hypotheses," Nathanial mused aloud. "Professor, would it be possible to visit these underground sections at Delphi?"

"Indeed, it would require some arrangements and permissions, but I believe it could be done. I can assist in facilitating this," Professor Demetriou offered, his own curiosity piqued by the potential discoveries.

"Thank you, Professor. That would be invaluable," Dr. Carter said, relief and anticipation mingling in her voice.

As their meeting drew to a close, Professor Demetriou provided them with copies of ancient texts that referenced astrological and mystical practices related to their sites of interest. Nathanial and Dr. Carter thanked him, their minds abuzz with new information and possibilities.

Stepping out of the museum, the late afternoon sun cast long shadows over the ancient city, mirroring the deepening complexity of their quest. The conversation with Professor Demetriou had opened new pathways of inquiry, not only into the physical realms of these ancient sites but also into the metaphysical and astronomical lore that surrounded them.

"Tomorrow's visit to Delphi could be pivotal," Nathanial said, feeling the weight of their impending journey.

"Yes," Dr. Carter agreed, her voice filled with resolve. "We're getting closer to understanding, Nathanial. Let's hope Delphi reveals more of its secrets to us."

As they walked back to their hotel through the bustling streets of Athens, the echo of the professor's insights resonated with them, blending with the chorus of the modern city around them. Each step they took was a step further into the labyrinth of history, guided by stars and scriptures long silent.

After their insightful visit to the museum, Nathanial and Dr. Carter arranged to meet with a local expert in Greek mythology and ancient rites, Professor Lena Georgiou, who was recommended by Professor Demetriou. They met at a quiet café near the base of the Acropolis, where the hum of the city created a lively backdrop to their discussion.

"Professor Georgiou, thank you for meeting with us on such short notice," Dr. Carter greeted, shaking hands with the professor, a middle-aged woman with keen eyes and a warm demeanor.

"It's my pleasure," Professor Georgiou replied, her voice rich with a welcoming tone. "I understand you are here investigating connections between celestial events and ancient Greek rituals?"

"Yes," Nathanial chimed in, laying out some of their research notes on the table. "We're particularly interested in how these rituals might relate to specific sites like Delphi and the Temple of Olympian Zeus."

Professor Georgiou nodded thoughtfully. "Ah, those sites are steeped in lore that ties directly to the cosmos. For instance, Delphi was considered the navel of the world, a point of cosmic significance. It's said that the site was chosen by Zeus himself by releasing two eagles from opposite ends of the world, and they met over Delphi."

"That's fascinating," Dr. Carter remarked, scribbling notes eagerly. "Does the lore speak to any specific rituals that might coincide with celestial events?"

"Indeed, it does," the professor continued. "The Pythian Games, held in Delphi, were not only athletic competitions but also deeply spiritual events that coincided with various solar phenomena. These games were said to honor Apollo's victory over Python and were marked by sacrifices and hymns that are believed to align with solar and possibly lunar cycles."

Nathanial leaned in, intrigued. "And the Temple of Olympian Zeus? Were there similar occurrences or beliefs tied to celestial alignments there?"

"Very much so," Professor Georgiou confirmed. "The temple was aligned so that on certain days of the year, the sun would set exactly between its columns, which was believed to be a sign of Zeus's enduring power and presence. Such alignments were often accompanied by festivals and offerings."

Dr. Carter looked up from her notes, a realization dawning. "These alignments and events... they might be what the scroll is referencing. It's not just prophetic; it could be a record or a guide to these important events."

"It sounds increasingly likely," Nathanial agreed, his mind racing with the implications. "Professor, could these ancient observations and alignments have been intended to influence or predict events, not just commemorate them?"

"That's a possibility," Professor Georgiou pondered. "The ancients believed that celestial events were messages from the gods. By aligning their rituals with these events, they may have been attempting to harness divine favor or insight."

As the discussion wound down, Nathanial and Dr. Carter thanked Professor Georgiou for her insights, which had added another layer of depth to their understanding of the ancient texts and sites they were investigating.

Leaving the café, the two researchers walked back through the bustling streets of Athens, their conversation turning to the next steps in their journey. The meeting had reinforced their theory that the ancient rituals and their timing were crucial not merely for their religious significance but for their potential to affect real-world events as suggested by the scroll.

"Tomorrow, we'll see these sites for ourselves," Nathanial said, a sense of purpose clear in his voice. "It's one thing to hear about them and another to actually stand where these ancient rituals took place."

"Yes," Dr. Carter agreed, her thoughts already on their upcoming visit to Delphi. "Being there might give us the final pieces we need to understand how these practices were linked to the prophecies and events described in the scroll."

As they continued their walk, the ancient stones of Athens beneath their feet seemed to echo with the whispers of the past, each step bringing them closer to uncovering secrets that had been hidden in plain sight for millennia.

The next morning, Nathanial Dove and Dr. Helen Carter sat together in the lobby of their Athens hotel, surrounded by maps, ancient texts, and various digital devices. Their planning session was focused and intense, a prelude to their journey to the heart of ancient Greek spiritual power, Delphi.

Nathanial spread a detailed map of Delphi across the table, his finger tracing the route they would take from Athens to the sacred site. "Once we arrive, we need to maximize our time. The key areas we need to explore are the Temple of Apollo, the ancient theater, and if possible, the lesser-known underground sections that Professor Demetriou mentioned."

Dr. Carter nodded, reviewing a list on her tablet. "I've arranged for us to meet with the site director when we arrive. He's aware of our research and has agreed to give us access to some of the restricted areas, which could be crucial for our investigation."

Nathanial looked up from the map, his expression thoughtful. "We should also consider environmental factors. Delphi is known for its complex terrain, and some areas might be difficult to access. We need to be prepared for a physically demanding exploration."

"That's a good point," Dr. Carter agreed. "I've packed some additional gear—torches, ropes, and climbing boots. Also, I've included environmental sensors and a portable GPS unit to map our exact locations when we document findings."

"Excellent," Nathanial replied, making a note on his own digital device. "While we're on-site, I want to focus on aligning our findings from the scroll with physical elements at Delphi. Any alignment with structures or artifacts could provide the direct link we've been searching for between the celestial phenomena and the physical site."

Dr. Carter glanced at her watch. "We have a couple of hours before we need to leave for Delphi. I suggest we use this time to go over our notes again, especially the translations Dr. Stanton provided. We need to be absolutely clear on what we're looking for—any symbols, structures, or possibly overlooked inscriptions that correspond with the scroll."

Nathanial acknowledged with a nod. "Let's also review the historical accounts of the rituals performed here. If we can match descriptions from the scroll with documented rituals or events, it could help us understand the purpose behind these alignments."

The two researchers continued to work in tandem, occasionally discussing a point of interest or clarifying a historical detail. As their departure time approached, they methodically packed their equipment, ensuring everything was in order for the journey.

Upon arriving at Delphi, the landscape unfolded dramatically before them, the ruins whispering ancient secrets carried by the wind that swept through the valley. The majesty of the site was overwhelming, with the towering columns of the Temple of Apollo casting long shadows over the sacred way.

As they began their exploration, guided by the site director, Nathanial and Dr. Carter were meticulous in documenting every detail. Nathanial used his GPS unit to mark specific points where the physical features of the site aligned with celestial events mentioned in the scroll.

"This section here," Nathanial pointed to an area near the temple, "seems to line up perfectly with the solar alignment we discussed. And according to the scroll, this was a significant convergence point during certain rituals."

Dr. Carter, taking photographs and making notes on her tablet, added, "And these inscriptions on the temple's base could be the ritual texts we've been reading about. They seem to describe the processional routes and the offerings made during the celestial events."

As the day turned into evening, the pieces of the puzzle began to fit together, forming a clearer picture of how the ancients had possibly used Delphi as a center for celestial observation and ritualistic power. The exploration was proving fruitful, shedding light on the profound connection between the heavens and the earth as interpreted by the ancient Greeks.

Tired but exhilarated, Nathanial and Dr. Carter made their way back to their temporary base at the site, ready to compile their findings and plan the next phase of their research. The shadows lengthened over Delphi, the ancient stones echoing with the footsteps of the past, as they continued to unravel the mysteries held tightly by the sacred site.

Chapter 5
The Cult's Shadow

Nathanial Dove and Dr. Helen Carter arrived at the ancient site of Delphi, where the rugged mountains seemed to cradle the ruins in a solemn embrace. The air was crisp, scented with wild thyme and the earthiness of the sacred site. As they walked towards the Temple of Apollo, the sense of history was palpable, the whispers of the Oracle seemed almost audible in the gentle breeze.

"Here we are, Helen," Nathanial said, taking in the sprawling ruins that spread out before them. "It's hard not to feel the weight of history here."

"It truly is," Dr. Carter replied, her eyes wide with the awe of their surroundings. "Imagine, this was the center of the ancient world, where people believed the god Apollo spoke through the Oracle."

They were met by Andreas Papadopoulos, a local archaeologist who had agreed to assist them during their stay. Andreas was a middle-aged man with a gentle demeanor and deep knowledge of Delphi's history.

"Welcome to Delphi," Andreas greeted them warmly. "I understand you are here to study the celestial alignments related to the prophecies found in your ancient scroll?"

"That's correct," Nathanial confirmed. "We believe there might be specific locations here that align with certain celestial events described in the scroll. These alignments could possibly shed light on the rituals and prophecies that were performed here."

Andreas nodded, understanding the significance of their project. "Many scholars have suggested that the placement of structures here at Delphi was deliberately aligned with celestial phenomena. The Temple of Apollo, for instance, has several architectural features that align with the sun during significant solar events."

"That's exactly what we're hoping to explore," Dr. Carter said, pulling out a map and some notes. "Can you show us these features, Andreas?"

"Of course," Andreas replied, leading them towards the temple. As they walked, he pointed out various archaeological markers and explained their historical context. "Here, you can see the remains of what was once the temple's pronaos. During the winter solstice, the sun's rays would pass directly through the temple's main axis."

Nathanial was meticulously taking notes. "And are there similar alignments during other parts of the year?"

"Yes, during the equinoxes, the light would illuminate the adyton, the inner sanctum where the Oracle was believed to deliver her prophecies," Andreas explained.

Dr. Carter looked intrigued. "This correlation between celestial events and architectural design suggests a deep understanding of astronomy."

"It does," Andreas agreed. "And it wasn't just about architecture or astronomy; it was deeply spiritual. They believed these celestial events were moments when divine energies were particularly accessible."

As they reached the Temple of Apollo, Nathanial paused to set up some equipment. "We brought some tools to help us verify these alignments precisely. If we can match them with the events described in our scroll, it could provide a new understanding of how the ancients used this knowledge."

Andreas watched with interest as Nathanial prepared a digital transit and other devices to measure angles and shadows. "This is fascinating. Your findings could add a significant layer to our understanding of Delphi."

Dr. Carter, who was examining some of the carvings on the temple's stones, called Nathanial over. "Look at this, Nathanial. These symbols might correspond to those in the scroll. They seem to depict celestial bodies and perhaps their movements."

Nathanial joined her, examining the carvings closely. "You might be right, Helen. This could indicate that the temple was not just passively aligned with these events but actively used as a tool for prediction or synchronization."

Their discussion was rich with technical details and historical context as they continued to explore and document their findings. Each piece of evidence brought them closer to understanding the ancient secrets of Delphi, drawing them deeper into the shadows of history and mystery that the site embodied.

By the time the sun began to set, casting long shadows across the ruins, they had gathered a wealth of data and observations. Returning to their temporary base at the site, they were filled with a sense of accomplishment but also a growing realization of the enormity of the task ahead. The secrets of Delphi were slowly yielding to their inquiry, yet each answer seemed to lead to more questions. As they prepared for another day of exploration, the mystery of the ancient site continued to unfold, layer by layer.

The next morning at Delphi, Nathanial and Dr. Carter, accompanied by Andreas, ventured deeper into the archaeological site. Their plan was to explore a lesser-known network of underground passages recently uncovered by local archaeologists. These passages, believed to be part of an ancient ritual complex, had not yet been fully documented or studied.

As they descended into the cool, dimly lit underground chambers, the air grew damp and heavy with the musk of earth and stone. Nathanial led the way, flashlight in hand, illuminating the narrow walls adorned with faint, barely discernible frescoes.

"This is incredible," Dr. Carter whispered, her voice echoing slightly in the confined space. "These murals... they could be contemporaneous with the period of our scroll."

Andreas nodded, equally awed. "Yes, and look here," he said, pointing to a series of symbols that resembled those they had discussed the previous day. "These symbols are thought to represent various celestial bodies and events. This chamber might have been used for specific astronomical observations or rituals."

Nathanial took photographs, ensuring they had records of all symbols and inscriptions. "These findings could be crucial in understanding the exact nature of the rituals performed here."

As they moved further into the labyrinthine network, the passageway opened into a larger chamber. In the center, a small, roughly circular altar stood, its surface grooved and stained with the patina of age.

"Could this have been where the rituals were conducted?" Dr. Carter asked, her flashlight beam circling the altar.

"Possibly," Andreas replied. "It's consistent with other ritualistic sites from the period. The alignment and positioning within the chamber suggest it was significant."

While examining the altar, Nathanial noticed something partially buried in the dirt floor near its base. He knelt down, brushing away the dirt to reveal a small, metallic object. "What's this?" he murmured, carefully extracting it from the ground.

It was a thin, bronze dagger, its handle intricately decorated with symbols similar to those on the chamber walls. The blade, though tarnished, still held a menacing sharpness.

"This isn't a typical archaeological find," Nathanial said, his tone cautious. "A dagger like this... it might have been used for animal, or even human, sacrifices."

Dr. Carter examined the dagger closely. "The symbols on the handle— are they the same as those on the altar?"

"Yes, they are," Nathanial confirmed. "This could indicate that the rituals conducted here involved elements of sacrifice, aligning the acts with specific celestial events to perhaps enhance their supposed power or efficacy."

Andreas, looking uneasy, added, "Finding such an artifact here isn't just significant archaeologically. It might also attract unwanted attention. Items like this are highly valued, not just by museums but also by those who might want to use them for... other purposes."

"You mean the black market, or cults?" Dr. Carter asked, her voice tinged with concern.

"Exactly," Andreas replied. "There have been reports of new cults trying to revive ancient practices. They often seek out artifacts like this."

Nathanial carefully wrapped the dagger in a cloth. "We need to document this find and ensure it's secured. It's too important and potentially dangerous to be left vulnerable."

"I'll contact the local authorities and the heritage office," Andreas said, pulling out his phone. "They'll want to secure the site and possibly restrict further access until we can ensure everything is properly protected."

As they retraced their steps back through the underground passages, the weight of their discovery hung heavily between them. The implications were profound, touching on historical, archaeological, and ethical dimensions.

"We should also consider increasing our security measures," Dr. Carter suggested. "If there are groups interested in these kinds of artifacts for the wrong reasons, we could be at risk."

"Agreed," Nathanial said, his mind already racing with the necessary precautions. "Let's make that a priority."

By the time they emerged back into the daylight, the serene beauty of Delphi took on a new, more somber aspect. The shadows cast by the ancient stones now seemed to hint at deeper, darker secrets lying hidden beneath the sacred ground, secrets that were intertwined with both the past and the present in ways they were only beginning to understand.

Later that day, as Nathanial and Dr. Carter reviewed their findings at a local café near the archaeological site, they were approached by a man introducing himself as Marcus Levant. He was a well-dressed individual with an intense gaze and an air of calculated charisma.

"Dr. Carter, Mr. Dove, I hope I'm not intruding," Marcus began, extending a hand, which Nathanial and Dr. Carter hesitantly shook. "I've heard of your work here and couldn't help but be intrigued."

Nathanial raised an eyebrow, curious yet cautious. "And you are?"

"Marcus Levant. I'm a scholar of ancient mystic practices and a consultant on cultural preservation," Marcus explained, his voice smooth and confident. "I understand you've uncovered something quite significant in the underground chambers."

Dr. Carter exchanged a glance with Nathanial before responding. "We've found several items and symbols that could be important to understanding the historical and astronomical significance of the site."

Marcus nodded, his interest apparent. "Fascinating. Delphi is known for its deep connections to celestial phenomena and its role in ancient rituals. But I must caution you, such discoveries can attract the wrong kind of attention."

"That's something we're becoming increasingly aware of," Nathanial admitted, watching Marcus closely. "We've already taken steps to ensure the security of the site and the artifacts."

"Very wise," Marcus said, leaning in slightly. "But it's not just physical security you should be concerned with. There are groups, cults if you will, who seek out such artifacts for their own purposes. They believe these items hold mystical powers that can be harnessed."

Dr. Carter frowned. "We are strictly interested in the academic and historical implications of our findings. We do not condone nor support any misuse of archaeological artifacts."

"Of course, of course," Marcus replied smoothly. "However, my concern is that your research, particularly if it's published or discussed publicly, might draw interest from these groups. They can be quite persistent and, sometimes, dangerous."

Nathanial considered this, his expression serious. "Do you have suggestions on how we might protect our work from such interference?"

Marcus smiled, a glint of something unreadable in his eyes. "Keeping a low profile is key. Also, working with local authorities and perhaps security experts who understand the unique threats associated with archaeological artifacts."

"We'll certainly take your advice into consideration," Dr. Carter said diplomatically. "Thank you for your concern, Mr. Levant."

"It's my pleasure," Marcus said, standing to leave. "If you ever require assistance or further consultation, especially regarding the protection of such artifacts, feel free to contact me."

After Marcus left, Nathanial turned to Dr. Carter, his expression thoughtful and slightly troubled. "What do you make of him?"

Dr. Carter sighed, watching Marcus disappear into the crowd. "He seemed knowledgeable, but there was something about him that didn't sit right with me. We need to be careful about whom we trust with our findings."

Nathanial nodded, his gaze lingering in the direction Marcus had gone. "I agree. Let's keep our findings between our trusted team for now. And maybe look into Mr. Levant a bit more. If he is who he says he is, there should be some record of his work."

As they packed up their notes and equipment, both felt the weight of Marcus's warning. The discovery at Delphi was not only a significant academic achievement but also a beacon that might attract those with less scholarly intentions. The conversation with Marcus Levant had added an unexpected layer of complexity to their expedition, reminding them that the shadows of the past could cast long and sometimes dangerous silhouettes into the present.

As the sun began to set over Delphi, casting elongated shadows across the ancient ruins, Nathanial and Dr. Carter returned to their research base, their minds burdened with the unsettling encounter with Marcus Levant. While Nathanial set up his laptop to do some background checks on Levant, Dr. Carter organized their notes and photographic evidence, ensuring every detail from their explorations was meticulously documented.

The quiet of the evening was occasionally broken by the clicking of Nathanial's keyboard and the soft rustling of paper as Dr. Carter flipped through her field notes. Each was absorbed in their tasks, yet the underlying tension from the day's revelations lingered palpably between them.

Nathanial's search yielded scant information on Marcus Levant, which only deepened his suspicions. "There's surprisingly little about him online," he muttered, frustration evident in his tone. "Just a few mentions here and there in connection with cultural preservation, but nothing substantial."

Dr. Carter, looking over from her work, frowned. "That's odd, given his claim of being a consultant in such a specialized field. We should definitely proceed with caution."

Their discussion was interrupted by a knock on the door. Andreas, looking more serious than usual, stepped into the room. "I've just received a call from the local heritage office," he began, his voice tinged with concern. "They've had reports of unusual activity near some of the less-frequented parts of the site. It seems someone's been asking about your work, particularly about the artifacts you found."

Nathanial and Dr. Carter exchanged worried glances. The news confirmed their fears that the discovery might attract unwanted attention, potentially from the kinds of groups Marcus had mentioned.

"We need to strengthen our security measures," Nathanial decided, his voice firm. "And perhaps it's time to form an alliance with the local authorities and heritage preservationists. We can't afford to take any risks with our findings."

Dr. Carter nodded in agreement. "I'll contact the heritage office first thing tomorrow. We'll offer to collaborate closely with them, ensuring our findings are shared securely and used to aid in the preservation of the site."

Andreas, reassured by their proactive approach, added, "I'll also arrange for more frequent patrols around the site and inquire with the local police about monitoring any suspicious activity."

With plans set for enhancing their security protocols, the team felt a slight easing of the tension. They spent the rest of the evening finalizing their documentation and discussing potential strategies for safely continuing their research.

As night fully enveloped Delphi, Nathanial and Dr. Carter sat back, the glow from their laptops casting soft light in the dim room. The challenges they faced had grown, intertwining their academic pursuits with concerns of safety and the ethics of archaeological discovery.

Yet, despite the complexities, their resolve to uncover the mysteries of the ancient site remained unshaken. Tomorrow would bring new challenges, but also new opportunities to forge valuable alliances and safeguard the remarkable history they were so dedicated to exploring.

The partnership with the local heritage office was set in motion, establishing a critical alliance that promised not only to protect their findings but also to enrich the understanding and preservation of Delphi's ancient treasures. As they finally turned in for the night, the quiet solidarity between them was a reminder of the strength found in collaboration, a vital counterbalance to the shadow of intrigue that loomed over their quest.

Chapter 6
Allies and Adversaries

With the early morning sun casting a golden hue over the rugged landscape of Delphi, Nathanial and Dr. Carter, along with a small team of local archaeologists led by Andreas, prepared to delve deeper into the lesser-known sectors of the ancient site. Today, their focus was on a recently uncovered section believed to be linked to the very rituals described in the ancient scroll they were studying.

As they equipped themselves with the necessary tools—notebooks, cameras, and various measuring devices—the air was thick with anticipation. Andreas briefed the team on the day's objectives.

"Our goal is to thoroughly document the architectural layout and any inscriptions we find in this new section. Given the potential significance of these areas, it's crucial we proceed with care and precision," Andreas explained, his tone a mix of excitement and caution.

Nathanial nodded in agreement, checking his digital recorder was fully charged. "We should also look for any signs of astronomical symbols or alignments, similar to what we've found in the main temple area. These could provide further evidence of how the ancient Delphians integrated celestial events into their rituals."

Dr. Carter, who had been reviewing their notes from the previous days, added, "I'm particularly interested in any artefacts we might uncover. Anything that could be directly linked to the rituals mentioned in the scroll could be invaluable."

The team made their way to the newly unearthed section, a secluded area of the site that was surrounded by dense brush and partially excavated ruins. The path was rough, and the air grew cooler as they descended into what appeared to be an underground complex.

As they explored, Nathanial took the lead in documenting the spatial arrangement, while Dr. Carter focused on the inscriptions. The walls of the complex were adorned with faded frescoes and carvings, some of which depicted celestial bodies and possibly astronomical tools.

"Look at this," Dr. Carter called out, shining her flashlight on a series of carvings. "These symbols are very similar to those in the scroll. See here, this carving looks like it might represent the constellation Orion, which we know was significant to the ancients during the winter solstice."

Nathanial joined her, examining the carvings closely. "You're right, Helen. And these markings below might indicate observation points or dates. This could be a key piece of the puzzle in understanding how they timed their rituals."

As they discussed their findings, Andreas sketched the carvings and took photographs from various angles. "These findings are extraordinary," he said, his voice filled with awe. "This section of the complex might have been an observational or ceremonial chamber specifically designed for tracking celestial events."

The morning passed quickly as they made several significant discoveries, including a hidden alcove that contained fragments of pottery and metal objects that may have been used in rituals. Each item was carefully cataloged and photographed.

"This alcove could have been where ritual objects were stored or consecrated," Nathanial theorized as he recorded their findings in his digital log. "The placement and the items suggest a direct use in the rituals, possibly during key astronomical alignments."

Dr. Carter, examining a metal fragment, agreed. "The workmanship and symbols on this fragment suggest it could have been part of a ceremonial blade or offering vessel. We'll need to clean and analyze it, but this is a promising find."

As the day drew to a close, the team gathered their equipment and prepared to return to their base camp. The discoveries of the day had provided them with new insights into the ancient practices of Delphi, deepening their understanding of how closely linked the architectural and ritualistic elements were to the celestial observations.

"This was a fruitful day," Andreas said as they hiked back to the entrance of the site. "Your insights have been invaluable, Nathanial, Helen. We're uncovering history that hasn't been seen in millennia."

Nathanial smiled, pleased with their progress. "And we're only just beginning to uncover the depth of knowledge these ancient people possessed. There's much more to learn."

Dr. Carter looked back at the ruins, her mind already on the next day's work. "Every stone, every carving here tells a story. We just need to listen."

The sun was low in the sky as they left the site, the shadows long and the air filled with the echoes of a distant past that was slowly revealing its secrets to those who dared to delve deeper.

The revelation of the artifacts and inscriptions unearthed at Delphi brought not only academic excitement but also unwelcome attention. The next day, as Nathanial and Dr. Carter prepared for further explorations, they were approached by two local officials, representatives from the Greek Ministry of Culture, who expressed an urgent need to discuss the security of the archaeological findings.

The meeting took place in a small office near the site, a room filled with the aroma of strong Greek coffee and the quiet buzz of an old air conditioner. The officials, Mr. Stavros and Ms. Antoniou, laid out their concerns in stark terms.

"We've received reports of increased interest in your activities here at Delphi, particularly from individuals with known connections to artifact smuggling rings," Mr. Stavros explained, his brows furrowed with concern. "It's imperative that we ensure the security of these artifacts. They are not only valuable in a monetary sense but priceless culturally and historically."

Nathanial listened intently, aware of the gravity of the situation. "We understand and share your concerns. We've taken steps to secure our findings and have limited information sharing to a need-to-know basis within our team."

Ms. Antoniou, flipping through a folder filled with documents and photographs, added, "While we appreciate your efforts, the ministry would like to propose an alliance. We believe that by combining our resources—our security personnel with your archaeological team—we can better protect these treasures."

Dr. Carter, thoughtful, interjected, "What would this alliance entail, exactly? We are, of course, eager to cooperate, but we also need to maintain academic independence and integrity in our research."

"The alliance would primarily involve security enhancements," Ms. Antoniou replied. "We would station guards at key points around the site and provide you with secure transportation and storage for any artifacts you deem particularly sensitive."

The proposal was sound, but Nathanial felt a twinge of unease, sensing the deepening complexity of their involvement. "And in return?" he asked, keen to understand the full scope of the agreement.

"In return, we would require detailed reports of all items discovered and, possibly, first rights to display these artifacts in national museums before they are sent abroad for further analysis or exhibition," Mr. Stavros said, his tone suggesting that this was not merely a request but a stipulation.

The conversation continued with Nathanial and Dr. Carter agreeing in principle to the alliance, recognizing the necessity of safeguarding their discoveries. However, both felt the weight of the additional oversight and the slight curtailment of their research freedom that this arrangement might entail.

After the officials left, Nathanial and Dr. Carter discussed the new development. "It's a necessary step, given the circumstances," Nathanial conceded as he sipped his coffee, his gaze lost in thought. "But we must be vigilant not only about external threats but also about the constraints this alliance might impose on our work."

Dr. Carter nodded in agreement, her mind racing through the implications. "We'll need to be careful about how we document and share our findings. Full transparency within our team and with the officials, but perhaps more controlled disclosures externally."

The rest of the day was spent in preparation, not just for the next phase of excavation but also in fortifying their camp and implementing the security measures discussed. By late afternoon, the site was buzzing not only with archaeologists and students but also with security personnel, a stark reminder of the treasures that lay beneath the surface and the lengths to which some would go to claim them.

As the sun set over Delphi, casting long shadows across the ruins, Nathanial and Dr. Carter reviewed their plans for the coming days. The excitement of discovery was now tempered with caution, the thrill of unearthing ancient secrets shadowed by the responsibility to protect them. The alliance, though troubling in its implications, was a shield against the darker forces that lurked at the edges of their groundbreaking work.

Under the guise of another serene morning at Delphi, tensions silently escalated within Nathanial and Dr. Carter's research team. They had begun to notice subtle discrepancies in their equipment setups and inventory logs. Items were not where they should have been; data seemed to be accessed by unauthorized users. It was a creeping unease that led them to scrutinize every aspect of their operations more closely.

As they reviewed security footage with Andreas, hoping to catch a benign mistake, a far more troubling scene unfolded before them. The footage revealed one of their trusted local assistants, a young archaeologist named Elias, discreetly pocketing a small artifact—a fragment of pottery with inscriptions that were crucial to their study. The time stamp on the video coincided with a brief power outage at the site the previous evening, a perfect cover for such an act.

The discovery was a blow to the team, more so because Elias had been with them since the early stages of the excavation. He had shown great enthusiasm and diligence, which made the betrayal all the more painful. Nathanial, Dr. Carter, and Andreas gathered in the privacy of their makeshift office to discuss the next steps.

"We need to confront him, but carefully," Nathanial stated, his voice steady but heavy with disappointment. "We don't know if he's acting alone or if he's part of a larger network."

Dr. Carter agreed, her usual composed demeanor tinged with anger. "Let's set up a meeting under the pretext of discussing his research duties. We can gauge his reaction when we bring up the security footage indirectly."

Andreas, feeling a personal affront, added, "I'll notify the site security to discreetly monitor his movements until we can resolve this. We can't afford to spook him into doing something drastic."

The meeting with Elias was arranged with an air of normalcy. The young archaeologist arrived, unaware of the suspicions, and was greeted by Nathanial and Dr. Carter with professional warmth. As they casually steered the conversation towards the topic of site security, Elias's demeanor changed subtly, a hint of nervousness betraying him.

When Nathanial mentioned the recent power outage and the subsequent review of security protocols, Elias's gaze flickered, and his hands tensed visibly. Dr. Carter, observing these cues, pressed further about the importance of safeguarding their findings. Elias faltered, his responses becoming hesitant and evasive.

Finally, faced with the undeniable evidence from the security footage, Elias confessed. He admitted to being approached by a private collector a few months ago, seduced by the promise of substantial financial rewards in exchange for small, supposedly insignificant artifacts. His role, he claimed, was never meant to harm the project but to help settle his family's debts.

The confession was a mix of relief and further complication. Nathanial and Dr. Carter assured Elias that the matter would be handled according to legal and ethical standards, emphasizing the seriousness of his actions but also offering a degree of sympathy for his plight.

After Elias was escorted away by security, the mood among the team was somber. The breach in trust was a stark reminder of the vulnerabilities inherent in their work, particularly when historical treasures were involved. The incident prompted an immediate overhaul of their security measures, including stricter access controls and more rigorous background checks for all team members.

As the day drew to a close, Nathanial and Dr. Carter reflected on the ordeal, their conversation sparse but meaningful. The betrayal had stung deeply, yet it had also reinforced their resolve to protect their discoveries. They were more determined than ever to ensure that the cultural and historical value of their findings at Delphi would not be undermined by greed.

The shadows that had fallen over their project were not just physical manifestations of the setting sun but symbolic of the darker aspects of human nature they had encountered. Yet, amidst this adversity, their commitment to uncovering and preserving ancient truths remained unshaken, a beacon of integrity in the murky waters of archaeological exploration.

In the aftermath of uncovering a traitor within their ranks, Nathanial and Dr. Carter found themselves at a critical juncture. The breach had forced them to reassess not only their security measures but also the broader implications of their project at Delphi. The late afternoon sun cast long shadows over the site as they met with Andreas and the representatives from the Greek Ministry of Culture to chart a path forward.

"We've tightened security and updated our protocols," Nathanial began, addressing the group gathered around a makeshift conference table set up near the site's command center. "Every team member has been re-vetted, and we've implemented additional measures to monitor and control access to sensitive areas."

Dr. Carter added, "It's crucial that we maintain transparency with the Ministry and ensure that all artifacts and findings are properly documented and secured. This incident has shown us the need for vigilance."

Mr. Stavros from the Ministry nodded in agreement. "We appreciate your diligence. It's unfortunate that such measures are necessary, but protecting these treasures is paramount. The Ministry is committed to supporting your efforts, and we will provide additional security personnel as needed."

Andreas, who had taken the betrayal personally, spoke up, "I've arranged for nightly security sweeps and installed new surveillance cameras at key points around the site. We won't let this kind of breach happen again."

Dr. Carter then steered the conversation towards the academic aspect of their project. "Beyond security, we need to discuss how we're going to proceed with the analysis and documentation of the new findings. The inscriptions we uncovered could significantly advance our understanding of the astronomical alignment and its role in the rituals performed here."

Nathanial pulled up a series of images on his laptop. "These inscriptions correlate closely with specific celestial events noted in our scroll. We're planning a detailed photogrammetric survey of the chamber to capture these alignments digitally."

Ms. Antoniou, also from the Ministry, was keen on the educational aspect. "Could we collaborate on a public exhibition or a series of lectures about these findings? It's important that the public understands the significance of this site and the ongoing efforts to uncover its secrets."

"That's an excellent idea," Dr. Carter responded enthusiastically. "Educating the public not only fosters a greater appreciation for cultural heritage but also serves as a deterrent against illicit activities. We could prepare materials and presentations that highlight the scientific and historical context of our work here."

The meeting concluded with a renewed sense of purpose. Each member of the team was aware of the challenges ahead but also of the unique opportunity they had to shed light on a significant part of human history.

As the group disbanded, Nathanial and Dr. Carter stayed behind to discuss the immediate next steps. "We need to finalize the setup for the photogrammetric survey," Nathanial noted, checking his notes. "And I think we should start drafting the outline for the exhibition and the lecture series. It would be good to involve some local historians and archaeologists."

Dr. Carter agreed, her mind already racing with potential themes and stories for the exhibition. "I'll start working on the educational content. And I think involving the local academic community will help strengthen our ties and ensure broader support for our work."

As they walked back towards their research tent, the site of Delphi quiet under the setting sun, the challenges of the day seemed to recede slightly, giving way to a cautious optimism. The path forward was clear, marked by a commitment to security, education, and rigorous scientific inquiry. Nathanial and Dr. Carter were more determined than ever to continue their work, fortified by the alliances they had formed and driven by the knowledge that each discovery, each piece of the puzzle they solved, brought them closer to understanding the ancients who had once walked these grounds.

Chapter 7
Clues from the Past

The morning at Delphi broke with the promise of revelations as Nathanial Dove and Dr. Helen Carter, along with their team, began excavating a newly identified section adjacent to the Temple of Apollo. The air was crisp, carrying the scent of pine from the surrounding woods and a hint of excitement as the day's work commenced.

"Over here, Nathanial, look at this," Dr. Carter called out, brushing away layers of earth to reveal a small, hidden alcove in the rock face near the temple's foundation. Her voice trembled slightly with anticipation as Nathanial hurried over.

"What have you found?" he asked, kneeling beside her to examine the discovery more closely.

"It looks like a collection of clay tablets, still intact," she replied, her hands deftly and carefully uncovering the items. "They're inscribed with what appears to be a continuation of the markings we found earlier."

Andreas, joining them with his toolkit, handed Nathanial a soft brush. "These could be significant, possibly records or additional ritual texts. We'll need to document everything meticulously before moving them."

As Nathanial and Dr. Carter worked to uncover and photograph the tablets, their conversation centered on the implications of the find. "These symbols here," Nathanial pointed out, "they seem to align with those we decoded last week. This could be a major breakthrough in understanding the sequence of rituals conducted here."

Dr. Carter nodded, carefully examining the inscriptions with a magnifier. "Yes, and look at this diagram—it resembles an astronomical chart. We might be looking at a calendar or a guide for timing their ceremonies according to celestial events."

The discovery sparked a flurry of activity, with team members carefully excavating around the alcove to ensure no further artifacts were disturbed. As they worked, Nathanial and Dr. Carter discussed the next steps.

"We should have these tablets transported to the lab for conservation and more detailed analysis," Dr. Carter suggested, recording their condition and coordinates in her field notebook.

"Agreed," Nathanial responded. "I'll arrange for a secure transport. Meanwhile, we need to expand the excavation around this area. There could be more to find, especially if this alcove was used for storing ritualistic items."

As the morning progressed into afternoon, the team uncovered several more artifacts, including ceremonial tools and fragments of what appeared to be ceremonial wear. Each find added layers to their understanding of the site's use and significance.

"I can't believe the condition of these textiles," Dr. Carter remarked, examining a fragment preserved against the odds of time. "This could tell us so much about the ceremonial practices and even the social hierarchy of the priests or attendees."

Nathanial, photographing a ceremonial knife with intricate decorations, looked up and smiled. "Every piece we uncover adds more depth to our understanding. It's like the ancients left these for us to find, to tell their story across the millennia."

By late afternoon, with the alcove fully excavated and all artifacts carefully cataloged and packed for transport, the team gathered to review the day's finds. "This has been one of the most productive days we've had," Andreas said, looking over the catalog. "The alignment of these finds with the celestial themes we've been exploring is unmistakable."

"Indeed," Dr. Carter agreed. "It's all coming together. Once we analyze these tablets and integrate their information with what we've already learned, we might finally unlock the full story of this site's celestial connections."

As the sun began to set, casting long shadows over Delphi, Nathanial and Dr. Carter stood looking over the site, a sense of accomplishment mingling with awe. "Tomorrow, we'll start with the detailed analysis. For tonight, let's document and secure everything," Nathanial decided, his voice filled with the fatigue and satisfaction of a day well spent.

The team nodded in agreement, each member busy with their tasks, preserving the past's voices so that they could speak once more, this time to a world far removed from their own. As they packed up under the fading light, the ancient stones of Delphi seemed to resonate with the echoes of discovery, holding still more secrets awaiting the light of the next day.

Back at their makeshift laboratory, a room filled with the latest technological equipment for archaeological analysis, Nathanial and Dr. Carter began the meticulous process of deciphering the inscriptions on the newly discovered clay tablets. The lab was quiet except for the soft hum of equipment and the occasional murmur of team members discussing their findings.

Nathanial carefully aligned the tablets under a high-resolution camera connected to a computer. "Okay, let's get these images processed. We need as much detail as possible," he instructed, adjusting the settings to maximize clarity.

Dr. Carter sat at the computer, analyzing the images as they came through. "These inscriptions are fascinating. They're similar to those we've seen in other parts of the site, but there are new symbols here that could be key to understanding their astronomical observations more deeply."

As Nathanial joined her at the computer, they both examined the symbols closely. "See here," Dr. Carter pointed out, "this sequence seems to be a lunar calendar, or at least part of one. These markings could represent different phases of the moon."

"That would make sense," Nathanial agreed, zooming in on the image. "The alignment with lunar phases could explain the timing of certain rituals. It's possible these tablets were used by priests or astronomers as part of their ceremonial preparations."

The team spent several hours analyzing the inscriptions, comparing them with other artifacts and records from the site. Dr. Carter carefully cataloged each symbol and its potential meaning, while Nathanial cross-referenced their findings with historical astronomical data.

"This symbol here," Nathanial noted, pointing to a particularly intricate carving, "appears to correspond with a solar eclipse. If we match this with historical records of eclipses visible from Delphi, we might be able to pinpoint the exact dates these tablets refer to."

Dr. Carter, scribbling notes fervently, nodded. "Let's pull up those records and see if there's a match. That could give us a precise timeframe for when these inscriptions were made and possibly for the events they were preparing for."

As they worked, the puzzle began to piece together, revealing not just dates and events, but a complex understanding of celestial mechanics possessed by the ancient Delphians. The team's excitement grew as each discovery offered new insights into the sophistication of ancient astronomical and ritual practices.

"Look at this alignment," Dr. Carter exclaimed after cross-referencing one of the symbols with astronomical data. "This tablet must have been created around 550 BC, a year when a significant solar eclipse occurred, which was visible from this region."

"That's incredible," Nathanial responded, his eyes wide with excitement. "It shows that they weren't just passive observers of celestial events but that they had a profound understanding of their implications."

As the day turned into evening, Nathanial and Dr. Carter prepared a preliminary report on their findings. The deciphered inscriptions provided not only a window into the past but also reinforced the importance of Delphi as a center of astronomical and religious activity.

"We need to present these findings to the team first thing tomorrow," Nathanial suggested. "Everyone should be aware of the significance of what we've uncovered."

Dr. Carter agreed, closing her laptop with a satisfied click. "And we should think about preparing a paper on this. The academic community needs to know about our discoveries."

As they packed up their tools and secured the tablets, the sense of achievement was palpable. They had managed to unearth secrets that had been buried for millennia, bringing them to light in a way that honored the scientific and cultural heritage of the ancient Delphians.

The next morning promised more work, but for now, Nathanial and Dr. Carter left the lab, their minds buzzing with the knowledge they had unlocked. As they locked the door behind them, the echoes of the ancient past seemed to blend seamlessly with the modern pursuit of understanding, bridging time through the language of the stars.

The following morning, as Nathanial Dove and Dr. Helen Carter continued their work at the lab, poring over the deciphered inscriptions from the clay tablets, an unexpected visitor arrived at the Delphi excavation site. Professor Lena Georgiou, whom they had met earlier in their journey, appeared with a keen interest in their latest findings and an offer of assistance.

Professor Georgiou, a specialist in ancient Greek astronomy, had heard of their remarkable discoveries through academic channels and had come bearing gifts—her extensive research on celestial alignments in Greek antiquity, including rare books and manuscripts that were not readily accessible online or in public archives.

"I thought these might help," said Professor Georgiou, laying out the texts on a spare table in the lab. Her eyes sparkled with excitement as she spoke, "These are some of my notes and translations of ancient texts that discuss astronomical techniques used by priests and astronomers during the period your tablets likely originate from."

Nathanial and Dr. Carter were grateful for this unexpected resource. The texts provided them with additional context and corroborated some of their theories about the tablets. They spent the morning discussing potential alignments and how these might correlate with documented historical events, such as eclipses and solstices, which were significant in the ancient Greek ritual calendar.

The collaboration proved fruitful. With Professor Georgiou's expertise, they were able to refine their interpretations of the inscriptions, particularly those that were more cryptic or ambiguous. The professor pointed out several subtleties in the language that they had initially overlooked, nuances that now seemed to indicate specific astronomical events with greater precision.

As they delved deeper into the manuscripts, they uncovered references to a rare alignment of planets, which was considered a powerful omen in ancient times. This event closely matched the date range they had established based on the tablets. It was a breakthrough moment—evidence that the rituals performed at Delphi might have been timed to coincide with this extraordinary celestial event.

The remainder of the day was spent integrating this new information into their ongoing research. Nathanial focused on documenting the alignments and updating their database with the new data, while Dr. Carter drafted sections of their upcoming report, which now included insights provided by Professor Georgiou.

By late afternoon, the team had mapped out a significantly clearer picture of how the ancient inhabitants of Delphi might have used astronomical knowledge to enhance their ritual practices. The implications of this were profound, not only for understanding the religious life of ancient Greeks but also for appreciating their scientific acumen.

As they wrapped up their work for the day, Professor Georgiou prepared to depart, her contribution having significantly advanced the team's work. "Keep me updated on your progress," she said warmly. "And do not hesitate to reach out if you need more assistance. This is just as exciting for me as it is for you."

"We certainly will," Dr. Carter responded, shaking her hand. "Thank you so much, Lena. Your help has been invaluable."

After Professor Georgiou left, Nathanial and Dr. Carter took a moment to reflect on the day's achievements. The unexpected assistance had accelerated their project, pushing them closer to a comprehensive understanding of the astronomical basis for the rituals at Delphi.

Their research was revealing a sophisticated integration of science, religion, and art in ancient Greek culture, a synthesis that resonated across the millennia, connecting the past with the present through the universal language of the stars. As they locked up the lab for the night, the weight of history felt a little lighter, shared as it was with fellow seekers of knowledge. They left the site with a renewed sense of purpose, eager to see what new revelations the next day might bring.

As dusk fell over Delphi, Nathanial Dove and Dr. Helen Carter sat down in their temporary office, a small tent equipped with maps, charts, and various archaeological tools. The soft glow of the lantern illuminated their determined faces as they prepared for a night of strategic planning. Their recent breakthroughs had accelerated the pace of their research, but also expanded the scope of their inquiries.

"We need to synthesize the data from today's session with Professor Georgiou," Nathanial began, spreading out the notes they had taken. "Her insights have opened up new avenues for our research, especially regarding the astronomical alignments."

Dr. Carter nodded, opening her laptop to access their digital database. "I'll integrate the new information into our existing framework. The alignments she pointed out could help us pinpoint the dates of these rituals with much greater accuracy."

Nathanial pulled up a digital map of the site on his tablet. "Let's also plan our next excavation phase. With our improved understanding of the celestial markers, we should re-examine sections of the site we previously overlooked. There might be more clues hidden in plain sight."

"As we expand the dig sites, we should consider more detailed geophysical surveys," Dr. Carter suggested. "Especially around the temple's eastern end. The ground-penetrating radar could reveal anomalies we missed during our initial surveys."

"That's a good point," Nathanial agreed, marking the area on the map. "I'll arrange for the equipment and additional personnel to be ready by the end of the week. We need to be thorough now that we know what we're looking for."

Dr. Carter then turned her attention to the logistics of managing their growing cache of artifacts. "We should also update our artifact cataloging system. With the influx of new finds, it's crucial that every item is meticulously documented and stored."

"I'll draft a new protocol for artifact handling and assign more team members to cataloging duties," Nathanial decided, jotting down some notes. "We can't afford any oversights or delays in processing."

Their conversation shifted to the preparation of their academic paper. "We need to start outlining our findings for publication," Dr. Carter mentioned, pulling up a document template. "This research could be groundbreaking, and we need to ensure our methodologies and discoveries are clearly communicated to the scholarly community."

Nathanial leaned back, thinking. "Let's allocate time each day to write sections of the paper collaboratively. I can take the lead on the sections dealing with astronomical alignments, while you could focus on the ritualistic significance and artifact analysis."

Dr. Carter agreed, typing a rough outline into the document. "That works. We should also include a section on the implications of these findings for the understanding of ancient Greek science and religion."

As they planned, their dedication to unraveling the mysteries of Delphi was evident in their meticulous attention to detail and their strategic approach to both fieldwork and scholarly dissemination.

"Once we have a draft ready, we should also consider presenting at an upcoming conference," Nathanial suggested. "It could be a good opportunity to gather feedback and engage with other experts in the field."

"Absolutely," Dr. Carter said, her eyes bright with enthusiasm. "I'll look into upcoming conferences and submission deadlines."

Their planning continued into the night, each task carefully considered and assigned. By the time they concluded their session, they had a clear roadmap for the coming weeks. The challenge was formidable, but so was their resolve.

As they stepped out of the tent, the stars were bright above Delphi, mirroring the celestial subjects of their research. The quiet of the night was a stark contrast to the busy day they had planned for tomorrow, but Nathanial and Dr. Carter felt prepared and eager to continue their pursuit of knowledge, guided by the light of both the stars and their scholarly ambition.

Chapter 8
The Cult Strikes

As the excavation at Delphi progressed, the atmosphere around the site became charged with a palpable tension. Recent discoveries had not only deepened the team's understanding of the ancient site's significance but also attracted unwanted attention that now seemed to loom over their efforts.

One crisp morning, as Nathanial Dove and Dr. Helen Carter reviewed the day's schedule, Andreas approached them with an urgent expression. "There's been a breach at the north perimeter of the site last night. It looks like someone was trying to gain unauthorized access."

Nathanial's brow furrowed in concern. "Was anything taken or damaged?"

"Not that we've found so far," Andreas replied, his voice tense. "But this is the second incident this week. We've increased security, but it seems we're dealing with someone determined."

Dr. Carter sighed, closing her laptop with a click. "This is exactly what we were afraid of. Our discoveries here are too important to fall into the wrong hands. We may need to consider even more stringent measures."

Nathanial nodded in agreement. "Let's review the security footage. We need to identify how they are bypassing our measures and strengthen those areas immediately."

Gathering in the makeshift security office, the team huddled around the monitors, fast-forwarding through hours of recorded footage. The breakthrough came when they spotted a shadowy figure moving with a cautious, practiced stealth near the perimeter fence.

"There," Dr. Carter pointed, "Can we enhance that section?"

The security team worked quickly to zoom in on the footage, revealing a masked intruder using sophisticated tools to disable one of the cameras temporarily. "They knew exactly where to hit us," Nathanial observed grimly. "This isn't just a random treasure hunter; it's someone who understands our operations."

The revelation added a new layer of urgency to their work. "I'll contact the local authorities and request an immediate investigation," Andreas said, already reaching for his phone. "We might also need to bring in a security consultant to overhaul our systems."

"Agreed," Nathanial said as he stood, pacing with a mix of frustration and resolve. "In the meantime, let's double our patrols and install temporary motion sensors at all key points. We can't afford any disruptions to our work."

Dr. Carter, meanwhile, pulled up a list on her computer. "I'll catalog all sensitive areas and items that could be targets. We'll implement a carry-in, carry-out policy for all artifacts starting today. Nothing stays on-site overnight until we sort this out."

As they implemented these new protocols, the team's morale was a mix of defiance and unease. The threat had made their mission all the more critical, yet it cast a shadow over their daily activities. Each member of the team was now acutely aware of the value and vulnerability of their work.

Later that day, as they walked through the site checking on the new security installations, Nathanial and Dr. Carter discussed the broader implications of their situation. "If someone is this determined to get their hands on our findings, it might mean we're on the brink of something even bigger than we realized," Nathanial mused.

Dr. Carter looked around the ancient ruins, her gaze thoughtful. "Or it means that what we've already uncovered has significant implications. We need to ensure our findings are published and shared responsibly. Securing our data digitally is just as important as securing it physically."

The sun began to set over Delphi, casting long shadows across the stones that had witnessed centuries of human endeavor. Nathanial and Dr. Carter continued their discussion, planning not only for the next day's excavation but also for a conference call with international experts in both archaeology and security.

As they left the site that evening, the heightened security measures—a visible reminder of the threats they faced—underscored the importance of their work and the need to protect it. The challenges were mounting, but so was their resolve to persevere, driven by the significance of uncovering history and safeguarding it for the future.

Under the blanket of night, with only the moon casting a pale light over the ancient site of Delphi, Nathanial and Dr. Carter were conducting a late review of the day's work in their onsite office. The recent breach had heightened their sense of caution, and they felt the need to personally oversee the implementation of the new security protocols.

Suddenly, the quiet of the evening was shattered by the sound of an alarm blaring from the northern perimeter of the site. Without hesitation, Nathanial grabbed a flashlight and headed towards the disturbance, with Dr. Carter close behind.

As they approached the area, they could make out figures moving stealthily among the shadows. Nathanial whispered urgently, "Stay back, Helen. Let me handle this."

But Dr. Carter was equally determined. "No, Nathanial, we face this together. Let's try to hold them off until security arrives."

Approaching cautiously, they confronted the intruders, who were now clearly visible as three individuals wearing dark clothing and masks. Nathanial called out firmly, "Stop right there! Security has been alerted, and the police are on their way."

One of the intruders, a tall figure, stepped forward, his voice muffled through his mask. "We just want the artifacts. Hand them over, and we won't have to hurt anyone."

Nathanial held his ground, flashlight aimed to obscure his face, creating a blinding effect for the intruders. "You won't find anything here. All artifacts have been secured off-site due to the recent threats."

Dr. Carter added, her voice steady despite the danger, "You're wasting your time. The only things you'll find here now are rocks and dirt."

The standoff continued, with the intruders hesitating, clearly not expecting resistance. The leader, growing impatient, took a threatening step forward. "Don't try our patience. We know you're hiding something. The tablets—where are they?"

Nathanial replied with calculated calmness, "As I said, nothing of value is left overnight. You've risked yourselves for nothing."

At that moment, the sound of sirens in the distance signaled the approach of the police. Realizing their position was compromised, the leader gave a sharp command, and the intruders turned to flee into the darkness.

Once the threat had retreated, Nathanial and Dr. Carter hurried back to the safety of their office, hearts racing but unharmed. They waited for the police to arrive, securing the site and ensuring no one else was lurking nearby.

When the police had conducted their initial investigation and left, Nathanial and Dr. Carter sat down, the adrenaline slowly ebbing from their veins. "That was too close," Nathanial exhaled deeply, the reality of the danger they had faced settling in.

Dr. Carter nodded, her expression grave. "We need to reconsider our presence here. It's becoming too dangerous. Our research isn't worth risking our lives."

Nathanial agreed, his concern palpable. "We'll discuss it with the team tomorrow. Maybe it's time to pause the excavation until we can guarantee better security, or until the interest in these artifacts dies down."

The encounter had shaken them, but it had also reinforced their resolve to protect the cultural heritage they were there to uncover. As they locked up for the night, the silence of Delphi seemed to echo with the echoes of past conflicts, reminding them that the desire for knowledge and power had always been a potent force capable of stirring both greatness and peril.

In the early hours of the following morning, as the first light crept over the rugged landscape of Delphi, an unexpected discovery prompted Nathanial Dove and Dr. Helen Carter into immediate action. Andreas, while inspecting the perimeter for any signs of disturbance from the previous night's intrusion, stumbled upon a hidden trail leading away from the main excavation site into the denser parts of the surrounding forest.

Alerted by Andreas, Nathanial and Dr. Carter joined him with a sense of urgency, equipped with backpacks containing necessary supplies and communication devices. "This could be how the intruders have been accessing the site," Andreas suggested, his voice low as they followed the barely discernible path, which was overgrown and easy to miss for an untrained eye.

As they navigated through the dense underbrush, the trail became more pronounced, indicating frequent use. The path meandered through ancient ruins that were less frequented by tourists and researchers, areas not fully excavated or mapped in detail.

"We should be careful," Nathanial warned, leading the group with a keen eye on the surroundings. "This area hasn't been fully explored. Watch for loose stones and unstable ground."

Their caution was warranted as the trail led them to a steep decline bordered by old stone constructions, part of the ancient architectural network that once served religious or perhaps even astronomical purposes. The historical significance of their surroundings was palpable, but so was the danger.

As they descended, a noise ahead caught their attention—a rustling that was too rhythmic to be caused by the wind. They paused, and Dr. Carter whispered, "Someone's ahead. Let's approach quietly."

The trail ended at a small clearing, where they saw two figures hurriedly stuffing objects into bags. The thieves, caught off guard, panicked at the sight of Nathanial and his team emerging from the trees.

"Stop! Drop what you're carrying!" Nathanial commanded, his voice echoing through the clearing.

One of the figures dropped the bag and sprinted deeper into the forest, while the other hesitated, seemingly torn. Dr. Carter, quick to react, moved to intercept the escaping figure, while Nathanial and Andreas handled the one who remained.

"We don't want to hurt you," Nathanial stated firmly. "We're just here to protect the artifacts. You can't get away with this."

The remaining thief, a young man with a look of desperation, finally dropped his bag and raised his hands in surrender. "I didn't want to do this. It's all gone too far," he uttered, defeated.

While Andreas stayed to guard the captured thief, Nathanial and Dr. Carter pursued the other, their chase weaving through ancient structures and over walls that crumbled under the weight of centuries. The pursuit was arduous, the terrain challenging, but fueled by determination and adrenaline, they kept close.

Finally, the thief, exhausted and unable to navigate the treacherous landscape efficiently, stumbled and fell near a secluded grotto, ancient and overgrown. Nathanial and Dr. Carter caught up, ensuring he was not injured before securing him.

"You can't outrun history," Dr. Carter said, catching her breath as she looked around at the grotto, the air heavy with the scent of history and damp earth.

The police were called, and the thieves were taken into custody, their bags revealing stolen artifacts that were thankfully recovered before they could be removed from the site.

As they walked back to their base, the morning sun now fully risen, Nathanial and Dr. Carter reflected on the surreal experience of chasing through historical ruins, an unintended yet profound journey through time and history.

"That was like something out of an adventure novel," Nathanial commented wryly.

"Yes, but let's not make it a habit," Dr. Carter responded, half-joking, half-serious.

Their return to the base was quiet, each lost in thought about the depth of their commitment to preserving history, not just through excavation and study but also through physical and immediate action. The morning's events had deepened their connection to the site, a tangible reminder of their role as guardians of the past.

Later that same day, while the adrenaline of the morning's chase still lingered, Nathanial Dove and Dr. Helen Carter returned to the site of their latest excavation near the Temple of Apollo. They were determined to ensure that no other artifacts had been disturbed or were at risk of theft.

As they meticulously inspected the area, Nathanial's hand tool clinked against something metallic beneath a loose slab of stone. With careful movements, he and Dr. Carter cleared the surrounding dirt and debris, revealing a small, bronze chest ornately decorated with symbols that resonated with those found on other artifacts from the site.

"Could this be what they were after?" Dr. Carter murmured, her voice filled with awe and curiosity.

"It's possible," Nathanial replied, examining the chest. "But it looks like they didn't manage to find it. This might be something entirely different, something they didn't even know about."

They decided to open the chest on site, ensuring any context found could be documented exactly as discovered. The lid creaked as it opened, revealing its contents: a set of small, delicately crafted figurines, each representing different celestial bodies, and a scroll made of a thin, bronze sheet intricately inscribed with what appeared to be a detailed astronomical map.

"These could be extremely significant," Dr. Carter said, carefully extracting the scroll with tweezers. "This map might give us insight into the specific celestial alignments celebrated or observed here."

Nathanial nodded, his eyes never leaving the figurines. "And these figures might have been used in the rituals themselves, perhaps as part of the setup of the alignment observations or as offerings."

The discovery prompted a thorough re-examination of the area. Under Nathanial and Dr. Carter's guidance, the team expanded their search, looking for any additional items that might have been concealed with the chest. Their efforts unveiled more fragments of pottery and inscriptions on nearby stones that seemed to narrate part of a ritual process, possibly explaining the use of the figurines and the map.

As the day turned into evening, and the shadows grew longer around the ancient ruins, the team carefully cataloged and packed each item for transport to the lab for further analysis. The site was secured, with new motion sensors and additional guards posted around the perimeter.

"Today has been quite eventful," Dr. Carter remarked, as they prepared to leave the site. "This morning we chased thieves, and now we're uncovering what could be one of the most significant finds of our careers."

Nathanial, locking the equipment shed, paused to look back at the excavation site. "It shows how unpredictable this work can be. But also, how every moment here is a chance to touch history."

Back at their base, as they prepared for the night, the importance of their work settled around them like a tangible presence. The new discoveries not only promised to advance their understanding of the ancient Greek astronomical practices but also underscored the ongoing threats to cultural heritage.

With the hidden relic now secured, Nathanial and Dr. Carter planned their next steps. They would need to collaborate closely with specialists in ancient astronomy and artifact conservation to interpret the scroll and figurines accurately. This work, while daunting, was invigorating, driving them to continue despite the challenges.

As they turned off the lights and secured the door, the site of Delphi lay quiet under the night sky, a silent witness to the day's endeavors. The past had once again made its presence known, offering new clues that connected the ancient world with the present, reminding them that their role as archaeologists was not just to discover but also to protect and interpret the whispers of history.

Chapter 9
Revelation at Delphi

After a brief sojourn to Athens to confer with additional experts and to secure more sophisticated equipment, Nathanial Dove and Dr. Helen Carter returned to Delphi, energized by the promise of new discoveries and the potential revelations the recently uncovered relics could hold. The sun was just beginning to crest over the mountains as they arrived, casting long shadows and bathing the ancient site in a warm, golden light.

The air was cool and crisp, filled with the scent of wildflowers mixed with the earthy aroma of the archaeological digs. The entire team assembled early, gathered around Nathanial and Dr. Carter, who were setting out the plan for the day.

"Today, we focus on integrating the new equipment into our excavation process," Nathanial announced, gesturing towards the crates of technology that had been shipped from Athens. "These tools will help us see beneath the surface without disturbing the ground, giving us a clearer picture of what lies beneath."

Dr. Carter added, "We'll also resume our examination of the bronze scroll and the figurines. The lab results have given us much to consider, and it's crucial we understand the broader context of these items within the site."

The team dispersed to their various tasks, with Nathanial overseeing the setup of the ground-penetrating radar and other diagnostic tools, while Dr. Carter coordinated with the lab technicians to ensure the delicate artifacts were handled properly.

As the morning progressed, the new equipment proved invaluable. The radar revealed anomalies beneath the surface near the area where the bronze chest had been found, suggesting there might be more artifacts or even structures hidden underground. Nathanial, examining the radar's output on a laptop, pointed out the irregularities to a colleague.

"See these shadows here? They don't match the natural strata we'd expect. We might have another chamber or perhaps a continuation of the passage network we uncovered last week," he explained, his voice tinged with excitement.

The work was meticulous and slow, as every signal had to be cross-referenced with existing maps and archaeological data to ensure they were not mistaking natural formations for human-made structures. The process was a dance of technology and tradition, as modern equipment mingled with old-fashioned tools like brushes and trowels.

Later in the day, as Dr. Carter was carefully examining one of the figurines under a microscope, she discovered minute inscriptions along the base that had been obscured by centuries of corrosion and dirt. "These inscriptions might be prayers or invocations," she mused aloud, documenting her findings with high-resolution photographs. "They could tell us more about the religious or astronomical significance of these figures."

As the sun began to set, casting a reddish glow over the site, the team gathered to discuss the day's findings. Despite the fatigue that marked their faces, there was a sense of accomplishment and anticipation. The new data from the radar had opened up additional areas for excavation, while the inscriptions on the figurines promised to yield new insights into the beliefs and practices of the ancient Delphians.

"We're just scratching the surface," Nathanial said to the group, his eyes sweeping over the ancient stones and the busy team members. "Every layer we uncover tells a story that's more complex and more fascinating than we anticipated."

Dr. Carter nodded in agreement, her gaze fixed on the horizon where the last light of day lingered. "Tomorrow, we'll start excavating the new anomalies. With any luck, we'll find more pieces of this vast historical puzzle."

The team nodded, their energies renewed by the promise of new discoveries just beneath their feet. As they packed up their tools and secured the site for the night, the stars began to twinkle above Delphi, silent observers to the ceaseless quest for knowledge that had driven seekers to these hills for millennia.

The next morning at Delphi, the excavation team, led by Nathanial Dove and Dr. Helen Carter, focused their efforts on the area identified by the ground-penetrating radar. The atmosphere was charged with anticipation as the team carefully removed layers of earth, revealing the contours of what appeared to be a hidden chamber beneath the surface.

"Look at this," Nathanial called out, his voice echoing slightly in the open air as he brushed away dirt from a stone edge. "This looks like a man-made structure. See how the stones are cut and fit together? This is definitely part of a larger chamber."

Dr. Carter, kneeling beside him, examined the stonework. "You're right. And the alignment—it seems deliberate, like it's oriented toward a specific celestial event. We might be on the verge of a significant find."

As the team carefully excavated around the revealed structure, the outline of a small doorway became apparent, partially blocked by fallen debris and earth. Andreas, joining them with additional tools, helped clear the entrance.

"Should we go in?" Dr. Carter asked, peering into the dark opening that now lay before them.

"Let's make sure it's safe first," Nathanial replied, directing a team member to check the structural stability. After confirming it was secure, he turned to Dr. Carter. "Okay, let's see what's inside. But let's be extremely cautious."

With flashlights in hand, Nathanial and Dr. Carter entered the chamber, the beam of their lights revealing an interior that had not seen light in centuries. The chamber was small but intricate, with walls covered in frescoes that depicted various astronomical symbols and what appeared to be a map of the night sky.

"This is incredible," Dr. Carter whispered, her light tracing the lines of the frescoes. "These must be the celestial events the ancients observed. Look, there's Orion, and there... that could be Halley's Comet."

Nathanial nodded, equally awed. "And over here, these inscriptions. They look like they might describe the events or rituals associated with these observations. We'll need to document everything and get translations started as soon as possible."

As they continued to explore the chamber, they discovered a series of small alcoves containing artifacts that seemed to be ritualistic in nature— ceremonial vessels, carved figurines, and metal objects that could have been used in observances or offerings.

"We need to get these artifacts out and start conservation work immediately," Nathanial decided, examining a metal object that resembled a celestial navigation tool. "Every piece could help us understand more about the purpose of this chamber and the knowledge of the people who created it."

"Agreed," Dr. Carter said, her gaze still fixed on the frescoes. "And these wall paintings are in remarkable condition, considering their age. It's a treasure trove of information."

After thoroughly documenting the initial findings, they carefully exited the chamber, ensuring it was secured against any potential disturbances. Back outside, the team gathered to discuss the next steps.

"We've just scratched the surface of what's in there," Nathanial told the group, his excitement palpable. "We need to organize a detailed study of the chamber—everything from the frescoes to the artifacts needs careful examination."

Dr. Carter added, "I'll coordinate with the lab to ensure we have the right conservation techniques ready for the artifacts. And the frescoes—we'll need specialists in ancient art to help us preserve and study them."

The discovery of the chamber promised to unlock new understanding of the ancient practices at Delphi, shedding light on the sophisticated astronomical knowledge and religious rituals of its inhabitants. As the sun set over Delphi, the team felt a profound connection to the past, a sense of uncovering secrets that had been hidden for millennia, now ready to be brought into the light of modern understanding.

Inside the newly uncovered chamber at Delphi, Nathanial Dove and Dr. Helen Carter, along with a small team of specialists, convened to further examine the intricate frescoes and the inscriptions that could potentially unlock more secrets of the ancient rituals performed here.

"Look at this section," Dr. Carter pointed out, her flashlight illuminating a particularly vivid depiction of what appeared to be a celestial event, possibly a solar eclipse. "The detail is incredible. You can see figures dressed in ceremonial garb, and there are inscriptions here that might tell us more about the significance of this event."

Nathanial, who had been closely examining another part of the wall, joined her. "Let me take a look. Yes, you're right. These inscriptions... they seem to be in an ancient dialect. It's going to take some work to translate, but this could be a major piece of the puzzle."

A specialist in ancient languages, Dr. Emily Stanton, who had been called in to assist with the translations, peered over Nathanial's shoulder. "I can make out some of this. It's discussing a prophecy... something about a 'shadow over the earth' and the 'alignment of the heavens'. This could indeed be referencing an eclipse."

"The ancients often viewed celestial events as omens or messages from the gods," Dr. Carter mused. "It's possible that this chamber was used to prepare for or respond to such omens."

Dr. Stanton nodded in agreement. "Yes, and these symbols here," she gestured to another part of the fresco, "they are astrological symbols. We've seen some of these in other parts of the site, but never with this clarity."

As the team discussed the frescoes and inscriptions, their excitement grew. Each symbol deciphered and each line translated added to their understanding of the ancient Delphians' astronomical knowledge and religious practices.

"This chamber could very well be a key location for the oracle's activities—perhaps even a place where predictions were made or rituals to interpret celestial messages were performed," Nathanial speculated, reviewing the images they had taken.

"That makes sense," Dr. Carter replied. "And given its hidden location and the secrecy surrounding its contents, it might have been reserved for the most significant rituals, attended only by the highest echelons of priests or oracles."

As they continued their examination, a quiet but steady rhythm of teamwork emerged in the chamber. Photographs were taken, notes were compared, and discussions flowed from one discovery to another. The sense of being on the verge of a significant revelation was palpable.

Dr. Stanton, who had been working on another section of inscriptions, called out, "I've got something here that might interest you both. This passage seems to be a direct invocation to Apollo, asking for clarity and foresight in interpreting an upcoming celestial event."

"That's incredible, Emily," Nathanial responded, joining her to look at the inscription. "It adds weight to the theory that this chamber played a central role in the oracle's predictions and rituals."

As the day drew to a close, the team gathered to review their findings. The chamber had indeed proven to be a treasure trove of information, offering unprecedented insights into the religious and astronomical practices of ancient Delphi.

"We need to ensure all of this is documented meticulously," Dr. Carter emphasized. "What we've found today could change our understanding of this site and its importance in the ancient world."

Nathanial nodded, feeling a deep sense of responsibility. "Tomorrow, we'll begin drafting our preliminary report. There's so much here to process, and the academic community will undoubtedly be eager to learn about our discoveries."

The team exited the chamber as the sun set, leaving the ancient secrets they had uncovered to rest in the quiet solitude of the night. They left with a profound sense of connection to the past, each echo of the oracle's voice seeming to resonate through the chamber, bridging millennia with the promise of revelations yet to come.

As the implications of their recent findings at Delphi began to settle, Nathanial Dove and Dr. Helen Carter convened with their team in the early evening to discuss the broader impact of their discoveries on the historical understanding of the site and its rituals. Gathered around a large table cluttered with maps, artifact photographs, and translation notes, the atmosphere was one of intense scholarly debate.

Dr. Carter initiated the discussion, her tone reflective. "The evidence we've uncovered in the secret chamber challenges some long-held beliefs about the practices here at Delphi. The precision of the astronomical knowledge and its integration into their rituals suggest a society far more advanced in certain areas than we previously thought."

Nathanial nodded in agreement, picking up a copy of their preliminary findings. "Yes, the integration of celestial events into their daily and ritualistic lives was not just about worship or divination. It appears to have been a sophisticated system of understanding and perhaps even predicting events that would have been crucial for their agricultural and social planning."

Dr. Emily Stanton, their linguistic expert, added to the conversation. "The inscriptions from the chamber provide a direct link between the oracle's predictions and these celestial events. It's as if they were using these occurrences to legitimize the oracle's power, or perhaps the oracle was using her knowledge to guide the city-state."

Andreas, who had been closely involved with the physical excavation, chimed in. "The architecture of the chamber itself is a revelation. Its alignment with specific celestial events—like the solstices and equinoxes—suggests a deliberate design, not just for religious purposes but for an empirical study of the skies."

Dr. Carter leaned forward, her eyes bright with enthusiasm. "This could mean that places like Delphi were not only religious centers but also early observatories, places of learning and knowledge transmission."

Nathanial, reflecting on the team's discussions, shared a broader perspective. "This shifts our understanding of ancient Greek society. They weren't just philosophically advanced, but also practically and scientifically. It makes you wonder what else we might be misunderstanding about ancient cultures."

The conversation then turned to how these findings should be presented to the world. Dr. Carter suggested, "We need to be careful about how we frame this. It's not just about adding a chapter to history but rewriting parts of it. The implications are vast—educationally, culturally, even politically."

Nathanial agreed, his voice serious. "Absolutely. Our next steps should include detailed papers for academic journals and perhaps a symposium where we can discuss these findings with other experts in the field. We need to be thorough and transparent in our methodologies and interpretations."

Dr. Stanton, who had been taking notes, looked up. "I'll start refining the translations further. The more precise we can be, the stronger our presentations will be. This is about setting a new standard in archaeological and historical research."

As the meeting drew to a close, the team felt a renewed sense of purpose. The discoveries at Delphi were more than just academic achievements; they were revelations that could change the understanding of human history.

Walking back to their accommodations, Dr. Carter mused aloud to Nathanial, "Imagine what the ancients would think, knowing we're still learning from them thousands of years later."

Nathanial smiled, looking back at the site shrouded in the evening light. "I think they'd be pleased to know they're still teaching us, still part of our quest for knowledge. It's a beautiful continuum, isn't it?"

As they reached their doors, the weight of their responsibilities mingled with the excitement of their discoveries. Tomorrow would bring more work, more debates, and further explorations into the ancient wisdom held within the sacred grounds of Delphi. The past was alive, whispering its secrets through the layers of time, and they were listening, now more attentively than ever.

Chapter 10
The Echoes of Oracle

With the excavation at Delphi yielding unprecedented discoveries, Nathanial Dove and Dr. Helen Carter knew that the next steps they took would need to be meticulously planned and strategically sound. Ensuring the preservation of the newfound relics and maximizing their research potential required careful coordination and forethought.

In the quiet early hours, before the site hummed to life with the day's activities, Nathanial and Dr. Carter sat in their makeshift office, surrounded by maps, digital imaging equipment, and piles of research notes. The air was thick with anticipation as they plotted out the logistics of their next phase.

Their primary concern was the conservation of the artifacts and frescoes uncovered in the secret chamber. Nathanial reviewed the list of conservation specialists and institutions with the necessary expertise to assist. "We need to ensure that the frescoes are stabilized as soon as possible. The fluctuating humidity in the chamber could lead to further deterioration," he noted, marking potential experts for contact.

Dr. Carter, meanwhile, was focused on the broader implications of their findings. "We should start drafting a comprehensive report for the archaeological community. This will not only document our discoveries but also set the groundwork for a more detailed analysis. We need to consider how we present our findings in terms of their astronomical significance and their cultural context."

The logistics of transporting some of the more delicate artifacts to more secure facilities for detailed study were complex. Nathanial outlined a plan for safe transport, including climate-controlled cases and security escorts, aware of the heightened interest in their work and the potential threat from artifact thieves.

"We'll coordinate with local authorities and our security team to create a transport schedule," Nathanial decided. "Each artifact's movement must be logged and monitored."

Dr. Carter nodded, adding, "And let's schedule a meeting with the local museum directors. They should be involved in the discussions about how these artifacts are preserved and eventually displayed. It's important that the local community benefits from these findings."

The discussion then shifted to the academic implications of their work. Dr. Carter proposed organizing a symposium. "We should consider hosting an international symposium here at Delphi. It would be an opportunity to bring together experts in archaeology, astronomy, and ancient languages to discuss our findings in a collaborative environment."

Nathanial agreed, seeing the value in fostering academic discussion and debate around their discoveries. "That's an excellent idea. We can align it with the publication of our preliminary report. It would provide a platform for interdisciplinary dialogue and help contextualize our findings within the broader scope of ancient studies."

As they divided the tasks between themselves, the weight of their responsibilities was clear, but so was their resolve. They were on the cusp of potentially redefining historical understanding of ancient Greek astronomical practices and religious life, a task both daunting and exhilarating.

The rest of the morning was spent in calls and video conferences, reaching out to colleagues across the globe, securing the necessary expertise and resources, and laying the foundation for the next stages of their project.

By the time they stepped out of their office, the sun was high over Delphi, casting sharp shadows across the ruins. The site buzzed with the quiet activity of the team members, each engaged in their work, unaware of the strategic decisions being made that would guide the future of the project.

Nathanial and Dr. Carter took a moment to survey the site, a sense of deep satisfaction mingling with the heavy burden of expectation. They were not just uncovering history; they were preserving it for future generations, ensuring that the voices of the past would not be lost to time but would echo on, resonant and clear.

With a clear strategy in place, Nathanial Dove and Dr. Helen Carter shifted their focus towards rallying support for their next major undertaking—the international symposium and the intricate process of artifact conservation. Their day was marked by a series of meetings, both in person at the site and virtually with experts and stakeholders around the world.

In the cool shade of an ancient olive tree near the excavation site, Nathanial met with local government officials and museum representatives from Athens. Dr. Carter joined them, her laptop open to a digital presentation showcasing highlights of their recent findings.

Nathanial began the meeting with a warm greeting, "Thank you all for coming. Your support is crucial as we move into a new phase of preserving and studying the remarkable discoveries we've made here at Delphi."

Dr. Carter took over, clicking through slides of the frescoes, artifacts, and sections of the celestial map they had uncovered. "Our findings not only shed new light on the astronomical knowledge of the ancient Greeks but also on their cultural and religious practices. We believe these discoveries belong to the world and especially to the people of Greece."

A local official, clearly impressed, responded, "It's truly remarkable what you've uncovered. How can we assist in ensuring these treasures are preserved and appropriately displayed?"

"We're organizing an international symposium, right here in Delphi, to discuss these findings with scholars from around the world," Nathanial explained. "We would appreciate your support in facilitating this event, ensuring that we have the necessary infrastructure and resources."

Dr. Carter added, "Additionally, the artifacts require immediate conservation efforts to prevent further deterioration. Collaborating with local museums and universities would provide the expertise and care these items require."

The officials nodded, discussing among themselves briefly before agreeing to assist. "We will provide whatever support you need. This is important not just for Delphi, but for our heritage as Greeks."

With local support affirmed, Nathanial and Dr. Carter moved to their next task—securing international involvement. They set up a virtual meeting with several prominent archaeologists, astronomers, and historians from various parts of the world.

As the virtual meeting commenced, Nathanial addressed the group, "Thank you for joining us today. We are here to extend an invitation to participate in our upcoming symposium on the astronomical and ritualistic practices at ancient Delphi."

Dr. Carter continued, "We've attached a preliminary report of our findings in the invitation email. We believe that your expertise could greatly contribute to a deeper understanding of these practices."

One of the invited experts, a renowned historian from the University of Oxford, spoke up, "I've reviewed your report, and I must say, the implications of your discoveries are profound. I would be delighted to participate."

Another expert, an archaeologist specializing in ancient Greek astronomy, added, "The celestial map you've uncovered is particularly intriguing. I have some data that might complement your findings and help clarify some of the symbols used."

As the meeting progressed, Nathanial and Dr. Carter fielded questions, discussed potential research collaborations, and confirmed several key speakers for the symposium. The enthusiasm was palpable, with many expressing eagerness to see the artifacts firsthand and to discuss their implications.

After the call, Nathanial turned to Dr. Carter, a look of relief and satisfaction on his face. "That went well, Helen. It feels good to have the international community's support."

Dr. Carter smiled, closing her laptop with a soft snap. "It does. It's reassuring to know we're not alone in this. The broader academic community's involvement will bring additional layers of insight to our work."

As the day drew to a close, the groundwork laid for the symposium and the conservation efforts instilled a renewed sense of purpose in the team. Nathanial and Dr. Carter looked over the site, feeling a deep connection to the past and a responsibility to the future, confident in the support they had rallied for the preservation and study of Delphi's new secrets.

In the quiet solitude of their research tent at Delphi, Nathanial Dove and Dr. Helen Carter sat across from each other, surrounded by ancient texts and artifacts, deep in discussion about the translations of the inscriptions from the newly discovered celestial map.

"This section here," Dr. Carter pointed out, adjusting her glasses, "seems to be some sort of guide or instructions. It's not just a map. The language suggests it was used by the oracles themselves, perhaps as a tool during rituals or consultations."

Nathanial leaned closer, intrigued. "A guide, you say? That could mean it wasn't just for recording or observing celestial events. Maybe it was a part of how they predicted or even manipulated political or social events."

"Yes, exactly," Dr. Carter nodded, her eyes scanning the document. "Look at this line here. It mentions the alignment of the stars with specific dates and events that were significant to the city-state. It's almost as if they used these celestial cues as a mystical guide for decision-making."

"That's fascinating," Nathanial mused, his mind racing with the implications. "It puts the oracle's role in a new light. They weren't just spiritual leaders; they were also guides for their people, steering them through uncertainties with the aid of these astronomical tools."

The conversation shifted as they explored how to present these insights at the upcoming symposium. Dr. Carter suggested, "We should structure our presentation to highlight this dual role of the oracles. I can compile the historical data on the political and social events of the period to see how they might align with our celestial map."

"That's a good approach," Nathanial agreed, typing notes into his laptop. "And I'll focus on the astronomical aspect, comparing our findings with other known celestial events of the era. It could help us understand the accuracy and influence of their predictions."

As they divided the tasks, their discussion was briefly interrupted by Andreas, who brought in a few more artifacts that had just been cleaned and catalogued. "These might interest you," he said, laying out a series of small bronze discs, each inscribed with symbols similar to those on the celestial map.

Nathanial picked up one of the discs, examining it closely. "These could have been used as portable aids or mnemonic devices for the oracles. See how each symbol corresponds to different parts of the celestial map?"

Dr. Carter peered at the discs, her expression thoughtful. "You might be right. It suggests these tools were widely used among the oracle's aides or perhaps even taught to apprentices. This could be a piece of the educational puzzle."

Their discussion deepened as they considered the broader educational practices of the time. "This indicates a structured way of passing down knowledge," Dr. Carter noted. "It wasn't haphazard; it was an organized transfer of sophisticated astronomical and ritual knowledge."

As the afternoon waned into evening, they prepared their findings for a small, informal presentation to their team, intending to test run their material before the symposium. The team gathered around, listening intently as Nathanial and Dr. Carter laid out their arguments and displayed the artifacts, including the discs.

"This guide wasn't just a tool; it was a part of a larger educational and predictive system," Nathanial explained, pointing to the projected images of the celestial map and the bronze discs. "These discoveries suggest a highly developed understanding of the cosmos and its impact on daily life and governance."

Dr. Carter concluded, "And so, the oracle's echo was not just spiritual or mystical but also a voice of knowledge and reason, guided by the stars."

The team's feedback was positive, with several suggestions to refine their arguments further. As Nathanial and Dr. Carter wrapped up the meeting, they felt a renewed connection to their work, inspired by the historical depth they were continuing to uncover. The echoes of the oracle's voice, once thought to be purely mystical, now resonated with the clarity of science and history, bridging the gap between the past and the present with each new discovery.

As the symposium approached, Nathanial Dove and Dr. Helen Carter gathered their team for a final briefing in their main tent at the Delphi excavation site. The air was tense, not just with the usual pre-presentation nerves, but also because of the increased security concerns following recent incidents.

Nathanial started the meeting with a clear, firm tone. "Everyone, as you know, we've had several security breaches over the past few weeks. We believe these were attempts to steal or sabotage our work. With the symposium tomorrow, we need to be more vigilant than ever."

Dr. Carter added, "We have coordinated with local and national security services to ensure our safety, but we also need to be personally prepared for any situation. It's crucial that we all stay alert and report anything out of the ordinary."

Andreas, who had been liaising with the security teams, chimed in. "We've doubled the security personnel for tomorrow and included strict access checks for all attendees. Everyone will need to wear their ID badges, and guests will go through a verification process."

Nathanial nodded, looking around at the team. "I know this adds an extra layer of complexity to our work, but your safety is our top priority. During your presentations, try to remain focused on your research. We'll handle the security aspects, but please, be aware of your surroundings at all times."

Dr. Carter then shifted the focus to the symposium's content. "Let's review the key points of our presentations. Helen, you'll start with the introduction to our discoveries, focusing on the significance of the celestial map and the newly uncovered artifacts."

Helen, one of the lead researchers, confirmed, "Yes, I'll outline our findings and emphasize the integration of astronomical knowledge into the daily and ritualistic lives of the ancient Delphians."

Nathanial continued, "After Helen, I'll discuss the implications of these findings on our understanding of ancient Greek astronomy and how this challenges previous historical interpretations."

Dr. Carter would conclude the presentations. "And I'll wrap up by discussing the broader cultural and educational impacts of our discoveries.

I'll also introduce the idea of Delphi as a center of not just religious but also astronomical education."

The team reviewed their slides and notes, ensuring each transition was smooth and that the data was presented clearly and compellingly. Nathanial paused, his gaze meeting each team member's. "This symposium isn't just about sharing our work; it's about demonstrating the importance of protecting such sites and the knowledge they hold. It's also a statement against those who would use underhanded methods to stop or twist these discoveries."

Dr. Carter looked around the room, her expression serious but encouraging. "You all have done incredible work under challenging conditions. Tomorrow is our chance to show the world the importance of what we do. Let's make sure we do it with the professionalism and passion that brought us all here."

As the meeting drew to a close, the team felt a mixture of anticipation and resolve. They reviewed their individual roles for the day, double-checked their equipment, and prepared their personal security measures—small alarms and communication devices that had been distributed as a precaution.

Nathanial ended the meeting with a call to unity. "Let's stand together, support each other, and make this symposium a landmark event in the history of archaeology and Delphi. We're not just defending our work; we're defending history itself."

The team dispersed to finalize their preparations, each person committed to the success of the symposium and the safe dissemination of their groundbreaking research. The weight of history was on their shoulders, and they were ready to face whatever challenges came their way. As they left the tent, the setting sun cast a golden glow over Delphi, the ancient stones a silent testament to the enduring quest for knowledge.

Chapter 11
Betrayal

The symposium at Delphi had attracted a wide array of scholars, historians, and archaeologists from around the globe, all gathered to delve into the recent groundbreaking findings Nathanial Dove and Dr. Helen Carter had unveiled. The morning was crisp, with a slight breeze that rustled through the ancient ruins, adding a mystical air to the already charged atmosphere.

As attendees mingled in the designated conference area, a series of black vehicles rolled up to the site. The arrival didn't go unnoticed; the cars stood out starkly against the backdrop of scholarly activity. Nathanial, standing near the entrance with Dr. Carter, watched closely as a group of individuals emerged.

"There's something off about this," Nathanial murmured to Dr. Carter, his eyes narrowing slightly as he observed the newcomers. They moved with a purposeful stride, their attire more formal and somber than the academic garb of the other attendees.

Dr. Carter, sensing the tension, nodded in agreement. "Let's keep an eye on them. Andreas, could you make sure they're checked in properly?" she discreetly asked their head of security, who was overseeing the entrance.

Andreas approached the group, politely asking for identification and the purpose of their visit. "Welcome to Delphi, may I please see your invitations and IDs?" His tone was friendly but firm.

The leader of the group, a tall man with a commanding presence, handed over a set of documents. "We are here at the invitation of Professor Dove. We have particular interest in the celestial alignments discussed in the symposium's agenda." His voice was smooth, yet it carried an underlying intensity that put Andreas slightly on edge.

Andreas checked the documents carefully, everything appeared in order, but he remained vigilant. "Thank you, sir. Please, enjoy the symposium. If you have any questions or need assistance, feel free to ask any of our staff."

As the group moved into the conference area, Nathanial pulled Dr. Carter aside. "Helen, I know Marcus Levant mentioned possible cult activities interested in our work. Could they be...?"

Dr. Carter looked thoughtful, her gaze following the group as they took seats at the back of the area. "It's possible, Nathanial. We should proceed as planned but stay cautious. Keep the presentations general, nothing about the specific locations of the new artifacts."

The symposium commenced with Dr. Carter giving an introductory speech about the importance of preserving historical sites and the impact of recent discoveries on our understanding of ancient Greek civilization. The attendees were captivated, but Nathanial noticed the group's keen interest, especially when the discussion touched upon astronomical aspects.

During a short break, Nathanial and Dr. Carter convened briefly with Andreas. "Keep an extra watch on them. Make sure they don't stray into restricted areas," Nathanial instructed, concern etching his features.

"I've already informed the team. They're under discreet surveillance," Andreas reassured him, his eyes scanning the crowd.

As the next session began, with a panel discussion on the implications of celestial alignments on ancient Greek religious practices, the mysterious group participated actively, asking pointed questions that skirted dangerously close to revealing their keen interest in the more sensitive aspects of the findings.

Dr. Carter, leading the discussion, handled the inquiries with diplomatic deftness, steering the conversation away from specifics and back to theoretical implications. "While we understand the fascination with these alignments, our focus today is on the broader impact of these practices on Greek society as a whole, not the exact methods or locations."

As the day progressed, the tension remained palpable beneath the surface of academic exchange. Nathanial and Dr. Carter communicated through glances and brief exchanges, their minds occupied with the dual task of sharing their research while protecting its deeper secrets from potential threats.

The symposium continued, a dance of knowledge and caution, as the shadows of the ancient ruins grew longer with the setting sun, hinting at the unseen dramas unfolding in their midst.

As the symposium at Delphi progressed, the tension that Nathanial Dove and Dr. Helen Carter had been managing beneath the surface finally came to a head. During a panel discussion on the integration of celestial observations in ancient religious rituals, the leader of the mysterious group, who had identified himself as Dr. Julian Moros, raised a pointed question that caught everyone off guard.

"Given the precision of the alignments and the sophistication of the tools you've described, isn't it possible that these sites were used for more than just observation? Perhaps they served a higher, more secretive purpose?" Dr. Moros's voice carried across the room, tinged with a knowing undertone.

Nathanial, who was moderating the panel, responded carefully, aware of the underlying implications of the question. "It's an interesting hypothesis, Dr. Moros. While there is evidence to suggest a variety of uses for these sites, our research is focused on what can be substantiated through archaeological findings and historical texts."

After the panel, Nathanial and Dr. Carter approached Dr. Moros and his group, determined to understand their interest and intentions. "Dr. Moros, your questions this afternoon were quite insightful," Nathanial began, his tone neutral yet firm. "May I inquire about your particular interest in the secretive aspects of these sites?"

Dr. Moros smiled thinly, his eyes sharp. "Professor Dove, Dr. Carter, my interest, and that of my colleagues, stems from a belief that historical interpretations often overlook the esoteric elements that could redefine our understanding of the past. We are particularly interested in how these might connect to contemporary practices."

Dr. Carter, sensing the conversation veering into sensitive territory, added diplomatically, "While academic curiosity is always welcome, we must tread carefully to ensure that our interpretations remain grounded in evidence and do not venture into speculation that could mislead or misinform."

Dr. Moros nodded, his expression unreadable. "Of course, Dr. Carter. However, we believe that sometimes, what is considered speculation might actually be an alternative perspective, waiting for validation. Our group, The Historical Enlightenment Foundation, seeks to explore these perspectives."

Nathanial exchanged a quick glance with Dr. Carter. This was the first they had heard of Moros's foundation, and it confirmed some of their concerns. "It's important that such explorations are conducted within the academic community's ethical guidelines," Nathanial stated. "We've seen the consequences when these lines are blurred."

As the confrontation cooled down into a more civil exchange of views, the underlying tension remained. Nathanial and Dr. Carter excused themselves, promising to consider Dr. Moros's perspectives but making it clear that their primary commitment was to credible, evidence-based scholarship.

Back in their temporary office, Nathanial and Dr. Carter discussed their next steps. "We need to be more vigilant, Helen," Nathanial asserted, his concern palpable. "Moros and his group are not just casual scholars. They have an agenda, and it could pose a risk to how our findings are interpreted and used."

Dr. Carter nodded, her mind racing through the implications. "I agree. Let's ensure that all our data, especially the sensitive information, is securely handled. And perhaps it's time to inform our university and funding bodies about Moros's interest. We need a united front in case things escalate."

As they prepared for the final day of the symposium, Nathanial and Dr. Carter were more determined than ever to safeguard their research and its integrity. The revelations about Dr. Moros and his foundation had added a new layer of complexity to their work, reinforcing the need for caution as they navigated the treacherous waters of academic and ideological confrontations. The stakes were high, not just for their careers but for the historical narrative they were helping to shape.

As the sun began to set over the ancient stones of Delphi, casting a golden hue across the site, Nathanial Dove and Dr. Helen Carter found themselves drawn into an unexpected and revealing conversation with Beck, one of Dr. Moros's quieter colleagues, who had lingered behind after their earlier confrontation.

Beck approached Nathanial and Dr. Carter near the excavation site, his demeanor suggesting a mix of hesitancy and urgency. "Dr. Dove, Dr. Carter, may I have a word with you both in private?" His tone was low, almost cautious.

Nathanial exchanged a brief look with Dr. Carter before nodding. "Of course, Mr. Beck. What's on your mind?"

Once they had moved away from the rest of the group to a quiet corner of their research tent, Beck seemed to struggle with his next words. "I feel it's necessary to explain why our group, and particularly Dr. Moros, has taken such a keen interest in your work. It's not just academic curiosity."

Dr. Carter, her interest piqued, encouraged him gently, "We appreciate your candor, Beck. It's important for us to understand all perspectives, especially those that could impact our research."

Beck sighed, looking somewhat relieved to be sharing his thoughts. "Dr. Moros believes that the findings here could validate certain... let's say, less mainstream theories about ancient knowledge and its applications today. He thinks that the celestial alignments and the artifacts could be proof of advanced ancient technologies or wisdom that has been lost or suppressed."

Nathanial, trying to keep an open mind, responded thoughtfully, "While we strive to keep an open dialogue about all interpretations, our goal is to remain within the boundaries of scientifically verifiable evidence. We've seen too often how speculation without basis can lead us away from the truth rather than towards it."

Beck nodded, acknowledging the point. "I understand that. And honestly, it's part of why I wanted to speak with you. There's a part of me that worries we might be pushing too hard for something that isn't there, or worse, misusing the data to fit a preconceived narrative."

Dr. Carter, sensing Beck's internal conflict, added, "It's a risk in any research field, Beck. The key is transparency, rigorous peer review, and staying grounded in the data. If Dr. Moros's theories have merit, they will stand up to scrutiny without needing to be forced."

"That's just it," Beck admitted, his expression troubled. "I'm not sure everything we do meets those standards. There's a lot of pressure to produce results that align with certain expectations or desires."

Nathanial, sensing an opportunity to foster a more collaborative relationship, offered, "Beck, if you ever feel that things are moving in a direction that compromises ethical or scientific standards, we're here. A fresh set of eyes, especially those committed to integrity, can be invaluable."

Beck seemed genuinely relieved, a hint of gratitude in his eyes. "Thank you, both of you. I may take you up on that. For now, just knowing there are others who prioritize truth over sensationalism is reassuring."

As Beck returned to his group, Nathanial and Dr. Carter discussed the implications of the conversation. "We need to be careful," Nathanial noted. "Moros's influence and motives could shape the narrative around our findings in ways we don't intend."

Dr. Carter agreed, her mind already turning over possible strategies to safeguard their research integrity. "Let's document this conversation and increase our vigilance regarding how our findings are presented and discussed, especially in public forums like the symposium."

Their discussion continued into the evening, both aware that the challenges they faced were no longer just about uncovering history but about protecting the truth of their discoveries from being distorted or hijacked by agendas that could undermine the very essence of their work. The stakes were high, not just for their careers but for the broader understanding of the past.

As the symposium at Delphi drew to a close, the atmosphere became increasingly charged, not just with scholarly debate but with underlying tensions that threatened to surface. Nathanial Dove and Dr. Helen Carter found themselves navigating not only the complexities of their archaeological findings but also the growing dissent among some symposium attendees, spurred by Dr. Moros's provocative questions and insinuations.

In a hastily called meeting in their research tent, Nathanial, Dr. Carter, and Andreas gathered to address the situation. "The dynamic is shifting," Nathanial started, his voice tense. "Moros's group is casting doubt among some attendees, questioning not just our interpretations but the validity of our methods."

Dr. Carter, equally concerned, added, "It's not just academic skepticism, which would be welcome. It's becoming confrontational, and that could undermine the entire purpose of this symposium. We need a strategy to handle this tomorrow during the closing sessions."

Andreas, who had been monitoring the crowd and the interactions, chimed in. "I've noticed groups forming, some aligning with Moros's views, others clearly disturbed by the direction of the discourse. We might be looking at a split, which could impact the final outcomes of this event."

Nathanial rubbed his temples, thinking through their options. "We need to reassert the scientific basis of our work. Perhaps we can request that the final panel be dedicated to discussing the methodologies explicitly—demonstrating the rigor and transparency of our processes."

"That's a good start," Dr. Carter agreed. "I can prepare a brief presentation on our archaeological methods, showing detailed steps from excavation to analysis. It will highlight our adherence to international standards."

Andreas suggested, "Should we also prepare for any disruptions? If things are getting confrontational, we might need to consider security measures during the panel discussions."

Nathanial nodded. "Let's keep that as a last resort but have the plan ready. The last thing we want is for this to escalate beyond verbal disagreements."

The conversation was interrupted by a knock on the tent flap. Beck stepped in, looking unusually flustered. "Dr. Dove, Dr. Carter, there's a problem. Some of Moros's group are planning to publicly challenge the findings tomorrow. They want to discredit the symposium's conclusions."

Dr. Carter sighed, her frustration evident. "Thank you, Beck. Do you know what their basis is for this challenge?"

Beck shifted uncomfortably. "From what I gathered, they're planning to use some controversial historical interpretations to suggest that your findings are being manipulated to fit a mainstream narrative. It's pretty thin, scientifically, but it could create enough doubt."

Nathanial's expression hardened. "We need to address this head-on. We'll use our closing remarks to reinforce not only the validity of our findings but also the critical peer reviews and checks they've undergone. Helen, maybe you can emphasize the collaborative nature of our project, involving multiple institutions and experts."

Dr. Carter nodded, already drafting points in her notebook. "I'll make sure to highlight the external validations and the ongoing studies that corroborate our findings."

"And I'll handle the security aspect," Andreas added. "I'll make sure there are no disruptions during the presentations."

As the meeting concluded, the team felt a mixture of determination and apprehension. They were prepared to defend their work, but the possibility of having to combat misinformation at a scientific symposium was a stark reminder of the challenges facing modern academia.

Nathanial looked at his team, his gaze steady. "Let's keep focused on the truth and integrity of our work. Tomorrow, we stand not just for ourselves, but for the principles of scientific inquiry and historical integrity."

With that, they each returned to their preparations, the night deepening around them as they fortified themselves for the confrontations that awaited with the dawn.

Chapter 12
A Race Against Time

In the shadow of the ancient ruins at Delphi, two parallel events unfolded, each marked by its own sense of urgency and significance. On one side, Nathanial Dove and Dr. Helen Carter prepared for the final day of the symposium, organizing their notes and finalizing their arguments to present a robust defense of their findings. Nearby, under the watchful eyes of Dr. Moros and his followers, a private ritual was about to commence, believed by them to realign modern understanding with ancient wisdom.

Nathanial and Dr. Carter met early in their makeshift office, surrounded by their research and presentation materials. "Today is crucial, Helen," Nathanial said, his voice low but firm. "We need to present our findings clearly and convincingly. We must demonstrate the scientific rigor behind our work."

Dr. Carter nodded, arranging her papers. "I'll start by outlining the methodologies we used, then I'll detail how each piece of evidence supports our conclusions. It's essential we leave no room for doubt about our integrity or the validity of our research."

Meanwhile, in a secluded area near the site, Dr. Moros addressed his group, their faces a mixture of anticipation and solemnity. "Today, we reconnect with the ancient wisdom that has been overshadowed by so-called modern scientific interpretation. Our ritual will demonstrate the power and relevance of the old ways."

One of his followers, a woman named Elara, spoke up, her voice tinged with reverence. "Dr. Moros, how exactly will our ritual counteract the mainstream narrative that has been presented?"

Dr. Moros responded, his tone didactic. "By performing our ritual according to the celestial alignments that we believe were originally intended for this site, we not only honor our ancestors' knowledge but also prove the effectiveness of their spiritual practices. This is about showing the depth of understanding that has been lost and must be reclaimed."

Back at the symposium, as attendees began to fill the conference area, Nathanial and Dr. Carter reviewed their strategy one last time. "We'll each handle specific parts of the presentation," Nathanial confirmed. "I'll address the archaeological aspects, and you tackle the interpretations and broader implications."

Dr. Carter agreed, "And I'll make sure to emphasize the peer-reviewed aspects of our work, the collaborations with various universities, and the ongoing studies that corroborate our findings."

As they spoke, Andreas approached, a slight frown on his face. "I just wanted to let you know, security is tight, and everyone entering has been double-checked. But there's a bit of a stir about Dr. Moros's group conducting some sort of private event near the site."

Nathanial sighed, a hand passing through his hair. "Thanks, Andreas. Keep an eye on that, please. While we respect their right to their beliefs, we can't afford any disruptions today."

In the distance, the sound of chanting began to rise subtly from the direction of Moros's gathering. The ritual had begun, with participants arrayed in a formation that mirrored the celestial map Nathanial and Dr. Carter had discussed in their findings.

Elara, deeply involved in the ritual, called out to the participants, "Focus on the alignment, let the energy of this place guide you. Our actions today will mark a return to truth, a challenge to the misconceptions spread by those who do not understand."

As the symposium officially started, Nathanial took the podium, his voice clear and resonant. "Ladies and gentlemen, thank you for joining us on this final day. We are here not only to share our research but to affirm the value of scientific inquiry based on evidence and collaborative scrutiny."

The dual rituals of science and belief progressed side by side, each set on altering the perceptions of the past, one through empirical evidence and the other through spiritual revival. The outcome of these simultaneous events would undoubtedly leave a lasting imprint on the legacy of Delphi, echoing through time like the oracles of old.

As the day progressed at the symposium, the celestial alignment that Dr. Moros's group had been anticipating was drawing near. This rare astronomical event, which they believed would lend power to their ritual and substantiate their claims, had become the focal point of their gathering.

Back at the conference, Nathanial Dove and Dr. Helen Carter were deep into their presentation, methodically laying out their scientific findings to a captivated audience. Nathanial was just concluding a detailed explanation of the site's alignment with celestial phenomena when Dr. Carter interjected, ready to transition into discussing the implications of these alignments on historical interpretations.

"Helen, could you elaborate on how these celestial events are not merely coincidental but were indeed significant to the ancient cultures we study?" Nathanial asked, passing the stage to her.

Dr. Carter nodded, her eyes scanning the room. "Absolutely, Nathanial. Our findings indicate that these alignments were intentionally utilized to mark important dates and events, serving both practical and ceremonial purposes. This wasn't random; it was a sophisticated understanding of astronomy."

Meanwhile, at Dr. Moros's gathering, the atmosphere was charged with anticipation. The participants were arranged in a specific formation, each person holding a replica of an ancient artifact, as they awaited the precise moment of alignment.

"Remember, everyone," Dr. Moros instructed, his voice barely containing his excitement, "the moment the stars align as they did thousands of years ago, we enact the ritual as it was meant to be performed. This will demonstrate the power and accuracy of the ancient knowledge."

One of his followers, a young man named Caius, spoke up, his voice full of curiosity and awe. "Dr. Moros, how will we know the exact moment? What should we expect to feel or see?"

Dr. Moros replied, "The alignment will be visible as the constellation directly overlaps with the marker stone we placed based on the ancient maps. As for what you will feel, expect a profound sense of connection, a clarity that our ancestors once felt."

Back at the symposium, Dr. Carter was taking questions from the audience. An attendee raised a hand, asking, "Dr. Carter, how do you ensure that these interpretations are accurate and not just modern projections onto ancient practices?"

Dr. Carter responded confidently, "That's a great question. We cross-verify our interpretations with multiple sources—archaeological data, historical records, and contemporary astronomical analysis. By using this multidisciplinary approach, we minimize the risk of bias and ensure our conclusions are as accurate as possible."

As the moment of the celestial alignment approached, both the symposium and the ritual reached their respective climaxes. Dr. Moros and his group began chanting in unison, their voices rising as the stars moved into position.

At the symposium, Nathanial wrapped up their session, "As we integrate these celestial events into our understanding of the past, we enhance our appreciation of the ancients not just as observers of the sky, but as participants in a broader cosmos."

Just as Nathanial concluded, an attendee interrupted, "I've heard there's a group performing a ritual based on these alignments right now near here. How do you respond to such uses of your research?"

Nathanial exchanged a quick glance with Dr. Carter before answering, "While we can't control how others use or interpret our work, we stand by the scientific rigor of our methods and the neutrality of our data. Our aim is to enlighten, not to dictate."

As the alignment completed, those at Dr. Moros's ritual felt a collective surge of exhilaration, convinced they had tapped into a profound truth. Meanwhile, at the symposium, the audience applauded Nathanial and Dr. Carter for their thorough and measured presentation, appreciative of the scientific insight that contrasted sharply with the mystical activities nearby.

The day ended with both groups feeling validated in their beliefs, yet standing worlds apart in their interpretations of the stars above.

As the celestial alignment reached its zenith, both the academic symposium and Dr. Moros's ritualistic gathering at Delphi were poised to assess the outcomes of their respective endeavors. Dr. Moros's group, still assembled in their ceremonial formation under the starlit sky, was the first to break their collective silence following the alignment.

Dr. Moros, visibly moved by the experience, addressed his followers with a tone of triumph. "Do you feel it? This is the power of alignment, the connection to the ancients we've been seeking. Our ritual has bridged the gap between past and present, validating the wisdom that has been lost."

Elara, one of the more vocal participants, responded with enthusiasm. "It was incredible, Dr. Moros. I felt a clarity, a sense of purpose. It's as if the stars themselves were speaking to us."

Another participant, a skeptical voice among the believers, interjected, "But how can we be sure this isn't just... psychological? The stars are constant, and our findings are subjective."

Dr. Moros replied, "While some of what we experience may be subjective, the alignment and its significance are not. These are based on ancient practices recorded and revered for centuries. Our experience tonight adds a layer of personal validation to the empirical data we've collected."

Meanwhile, back at the symposium, Nathanial Dove and Dr. Helen Carter were discussing the implications of their successful presentation with some of the attendees.

A curious scholar from the audience approached them, asking, "Dr. Dove, Dr. Carter, given the ritual that coincided with your symposium, do you think there's room to explore more interdisciplinary studies between archaeology and cultural anthropology or even experimental archaeology?"

Nathanial responded thoughtfully, "Absolutely. Understanding the full scope of ancient practices often requires us to cross traditional academic boundaries. What we advocate for is a rigorous, evidence-based approach to these studies, ensuring that we respect both the scientific method and the cultural significance of our findings."

Dr. Carter added, "It's about balance. While we must be cautious not to lend credibility to unverified claims, we also mustn't dismiss the cultural and historical contexts that these practices illuminate."

As the discussions unfolded, news of the ritual's emotional impact began to filter through to the symposium attendees, sparking a mix of curiosity and skepticism.

One attendee, intrigued, asked Nathanial, "Do you think such rituals, despite their lack of scientific backing, could contribute to our understanding of ancient belief systems?"

Nathanial replied, "They could, to an extent. Observing modern recreations of ancient rituals can provide insights into the ceremonial aspects of those practices, though we must always be wary of anachronisms and cultural misinterpretations. Our goal should be to use these observations as supplementary data, not conclusive evidence."

As the night drew to a close, both groups reflected on their experiences. Dr. Moros and his followers felt a renewed commitment to their cause, bolstered by their emotional and spiritual experiences during the alignment. In contrast, Nathanial, Dr. Carter, and the symposium attendees were reaffirmed in their commitment to empirical research, recognizing the value of interdisciplinary approaches but remaining anchored in scientific rigor.

The outcomes of both the ritual and the symposium highlighted a fundamental divide in approaches to historical interpretation—one deeply rooted in belief and the other in proof. Yet, both were searching for a connection to the past, a way to make sense of the silent stones of Delphi that stood as mute witnesses to the unfolding dramas of belief, science, and the quest for understanding.

The final day of the symposium at Delphi arrived with a palpable sense of culmination. Both Nathanial Dove and Dr. Helen Carter felt the weight of the previous day's discussions and the emotional fervor from Dr. Moros's ritual as they prepared for what was anticipated to be a pivotal series of closing remarks.

Gathered in the main hall, filled with academics, enthusiasts, and skeptics alike, Nathanial and Dr. Carter were approached by Dr. Moros and his group before the session began. The encounter was polite but charged with underlying tensions.

"Dr. Dove, Dr. Carter," Dr. Moros began, extending a hand, which Nathanial and Dr. Carter accepted. "Yesterday was quite revealing. I believe both our approaches have merit, and perhaps there is more common ground than we thought."

Dr. Carter, always diplomatic, responded, "Dr. Moros, we appreciate your insights and the passion your group brings to these discussions. Understanding ancient practices can benefit from multiple perspectives, though we must adhere to stringent research methodologies."

Dr. Moros nodded, his expression thoughtful. "Indeed, Dr. Carter. However, I propose a public discussion—now, in front of our peers—to debate our differing interpretations. It could be enlightening for all involved."

Nathanial, sensing both opportunity and risk, agreed. "Let's keep the discussion focused on the facts and the evidence. We're all here to learn and to share knowledge responsibly."

As the debate commenced, the audience listened intently. Dr. Moros presented his perspective first, arguing for a more mystical interpretation of the archaeological findings.

"The alignment we observed and participated in last night," Dr. Moros explained, "demonstrates that ancient practices were not only about observing celestial events but about experiencing them as transformative, spiritual phenomena."

Nathanial responded, "While the experiential aspect is undeniable, our responsibility as scholars is to differentiate between experience and empirical evidence. The alignments are scientifically notable, yes, but their interpretation must be grounded in verifiable data."

Dr. Carter added, "And while these experiences are valuable, they cannot define our methodologies. Our approach must be replicable and transparent, adhering to the academic standards that govern our fields."

The discussion shifted to the implications of these interpretations for modern understanding of ancient cultures. Audience members asked probing questions, challenging both sides, seeking clarity on the fine line between historical interpretation and modern reenactment.

As the debate drew to a close, Dr. Moros conceded, "Perhaps there is a need for a more integrated approach that respects both the empirical and the experiential."

Dr. Carter agreed, "Indeed, Dr. Moros. This symposium has shown us the importance of dialogue between different schools of thought. Let's continue this conversation, ensuring it is both rigorous and respectful."

The closing remarks by Nathanial and Dr. Carter emphasized the symposium's role in fostering scholarly debate and advancing the understanding of ancient practices through collaborative effort.

"This event," Nathanial concluded, "has not only been about sharing findings but about challenging our preconceptions and learning from each other. We thank all participants for their contributions and look forward to future collaborations."

The symposium ended with applause, a sense of achievement mingling with the realization that the journey of discovery was far from over. The day marked a turning point, not only in how the findings from Delphi were perceived but also in how diverse interpretative frameworks could coexist, each pushing the boundaries of understanding in their own way.

As the crowd dispersed, Nathanial and Dr. Carter felt a renewed sense of purpose. The challenges they faced had broadened their perspectives, and they were more determined than ever to continue their work, guided by both the light of the stars and the rigor of scientific inquiry.

Chapter 13
Gathering Forces

The symposium had concluded, leaving the ancient site of Delphi quieter than it had been for days. Nathanial Dove and Dr. Helen Carter took a moment to reflect on the events that had unfolded. They walked through the quieter parts of the excavation site, their path illuminated by the soft glow of the setting sun.

"That was quite a symposium, Helen," Nathanial remarked, his voice a mixture of exhaustion and satisfaction. "I think we managed to navigate through the challenges better than I expected."

Dr. Carter nodded, looking thoughtful. "Yes, I agree. It was a test of our resolve and our commitment to scientific integrity. But I think it also highlighted the importance of being open to dialogue, even when the perspectives presented are vastly different from our own."

Nathanial paused, looking over the ruins. "Do you think we managed to change any minds? Or at least, open some eyes to the complexity of interpreting archaeological findings?"

Dr. Carter sighed lightly. "Perhaps. If nothing else, we demonstrated that robust debate is a vital part of academic discourse. And maybe we've shown that there's a middle ground between dismissing non-traditional interpretations outright and embracing them without critical analysis."

As they walked, Andreas joined them, his expression more relaxed than it had been in days. "I must say, I'm impressed with how you both handled the pressures. Especially with the Moros group trying to push their agenda so forcefully."

Nathanial chuckled dryly. "It was certainly a challenge. But having solid, empirical data on our side helped. How do you think the security measures held up?"

Andreas nodded. "They did well. We were prepared for more direct confrontations, but thankfully, it didn't come to that. Moving forward, we'll need to maintain a high level of security, especially with the attention the symposium has brought us."

Dr. Carter glanced back towards the conference area, now quiet. "What about the local community and the officials? How have they reacted to the outcomes of the symposium?"

"They seem pleased," Andreas responded. "The spotlight on Delphi, if managed well, can boost both tourism and funding for further excavations and preservation efforts. They're quite supportive of continuing our work here."

Nathanial nodded appreciatively. "That's good to hear. We'll need to ensure that any increase in visitor numbers doesn't affect the integrity of the site. Perhaps it's time to discuss new strategies for site management and preservation."

Dr. Carter agreed. "Absolutely. The last thing we want is for this place to suffer from its own popularity. We need to advocate for sustainable practices that protect and preserve, not just for now but for future generations."

The conversation turned towards future projects as they reached a particularly well-preserved section of the site. "Looking ahead," Nathanial started, "we should consider expanding our research to include more interdisciplinary studies. Perhaps bringing in experts in ancient religions and cultural practices could help us understand the broader context of our findings."

Dr. Carter smiled, her enthusiasm evident. "I like that idea. It could really broaden the scope of our research and potentially lead to more nuanced interpretations of the data. Maybe it's time to start drafting some proposals for new research projects."

As they continued their walk, the shadows lengthened, and the site took on a serene, timeless quality. The challenges of the symposium seemed to fade into the background, replaced by a renewed focus on the future and the endless possibilities it held.

"Whatever comes next," Nathanial said, looking out over Delphi, "I believe we're ready for it. Today, we've proven that we can handle the pressure and turn it into an opportunity for growth and learning."

Dr. Carter nodded, her gaze lingering on the ancient stones that had witnessed centuries of human history. "Yes, we're ready. And we'll do it together, as a team, committed to uncovering the past and protecting it for the future."

As they returned to their base, the site quiet except for the soft rustling of leaves and the distant calls of night birds, there was a sense of completion, but also of new beginnings. The symposium was over, but the work would go on, driven by curiosity, dedication, and a profound respect for the ancient mysteries of Delphi.

In the aftermath of the symposium, as the dust settled over the archaeological site at Delphi, Nathanial Dove and Dr. Helen Carter realized the scope of their project was expanding. The newfound interest and subsequent funding boost presented an opportune moment to strengthen their research team. The process of identifying and recruiting new team members was approached with a strategic mindset, aiming to fill gaps in expertise and enhance the project's interdisciplinary approach.

Nathanial spent the morning poring over potential candidates, reviewing CVs, and research papers. He focused on finding individuals who not only had the necessary academic qualifications but who also showed a capacity for innovative thinking and collaborative work. His list included experts in ancient languages, cultural anthropology, and conservation science, fields that would deepen the team's ability to interpret the complex data they were uncovering.

Meanwhile, Dr. Carter set up meetings with various universities and research institutions. She discussed potential partnerships and joint ventures that could provide both human resources and technological support for their expanded operations. During a video conference with a prominent university's archaeology department chair, she outlined the vision for the next phase of the Delphi project.

"We're looking to build a coalition of experts that can help us explore not just the archaeological aspects, but also the cultural, astronomical, and even environmental impacts of ancient practices," Dr. Carter explained, her screen filled with charts and data from their recent findings. "We believe this holistic approach will not only enhance our understanding of the site but also contribute to a broader academic discourse."

The university representative was receptive. "This sounds like a groundbreaking approach, Dr. Carter. We have a couple of post-docs who are working on similar intersections. Perhaps we could arrange a collaboration."

"That would be excellent," Dr. Carter responded, jotting down notes. "We also value the integration of new technologies in archaeology. Any expertise your team can bring in digital mapping or remote sensing would be invaluable."

As the day progressed, Nathanial and Dr. Carter convened to consolidate their findings and plan the team's expansion. They discussed each candidate and potential partner, weighing their expertise against the project's needs.

Nathanial looked over the list, thoughtful. "I think Dr. Linh Nguyen from the Sorbonne should be at the top of our list for the cultural anthropology role. Her work on ancient religious practices in the Mediterranean is exactly what we need."

Dr. Carter agreed, adding, "And for conservation, I suggest reaching out to Dr. Marco Silva. His methods in preserving ancient frescoes could be crucial for our next steps, especially considering the condition of some artifacts we've unearthed."

They also agreed on initiating an internship program to involve younger scholars and students in the project, providing them with hands-on experience while contributing to the team's diversity and vitality.

"Let's make sure we're not just bringing in expertise, but also new perspectives. It's these fresh ideas that often lead to breakthroughs in fields like ours," Dr. Carter noted.

As the sun began to set over Delphi, the plans for expanding the team took shape. Nathanial and Dr. Carter felt a renewed sense of purpose, energized by the prospect of not only discovering more about the past but also training the next generation of archaeologists.

Their discussion continued into the evening, under the soft glow of lamps in their research tent, surrounded by maps and artifacts—a reminder of the tangible history they were working so hard to uncover and preserve. The quiet of the site around them was a sharp contrast to the flurry of planning and anticipation that filled their temporary workspace. The team at Delphi was growing, and with it, the potential to deepen humanity's understanding of its own history.

In response to the expanding scope of their project at Delphi, Nathanial Dove and Dr. Helen Carter recognized the need for more sophisticated tools to manage the wealth of data they were accumulating. The introduction of advanced technology was imperative to enhance their analysis and preservation efforts, and they were proactive in integrating these new resources.

Nathanial had been exploring options for digital mapping and 3D modeling tools that could provide more detailed visualizations of the excavation sites. He had arranged a meeting with a tech company known for its innovative approaches to archaeological applications. Sitting in his temporary office, surrounded by site maps and excavation photos, he engaged in a virtual demonstration with the company's representatives.

"We are particularly interested in tools that can help us create detailed 3D models of the dig sites, incorporating both the physical and historical data we've collected," Nathanial explained, sharing his screen to show the areas of interest.

The tech company's lead engineer presented a new software suite designed for archaeological use. "Our system not only allows for 3D modeling but also integrates with GIS to provide real-time data overlays. You can track excavation progress, catalog finds, and even simulate changes to the site over time."

Nathanial was impressed. "This could significantly enhance our ability to visualize the ancient structures as they might have appeared in their prime. It could also help us in planning our digs more effectively, minimizing disruptions to the site."

Meanwhile, Dr. Carter was focused on the conservation side of their toolkit. She met with specialists in conservation technology who introduced her to a new, non-invasive preservation technique that utilized nanomaterials to stabilize and protect delicate artifacts from environmental damage.

During her meeting, Dr. Carter examined samples of artifacts treated with the technology. "How robust is this method in terms of long-term preservation? Our finds are often exposed to harsh environmental conditions almost immediately upon excavation."

The specialist assured her, "Our tests show significant resistance to weathering and environmental stress. Plus, the treatment is fully reversible, which is a critical consideration for archaeological applications."

Pleased with the potential these new tools offered, Nathanial and Dr. Carter convened to discuss integrating these technologies into their project. They planned training sessions for their team and drafted protocols for the use of these new systems.

"Implementing these tools will require some training, but I believe it will be worth the investment," Nathanial noted. "Especially the 3D modeling software, which could revolutionize how we document and share our findings."

Dr. Carter agreed, adding, "And the conservation technologies will ensure that once we uncover artifacts, we can preserve them with greater efficacy. It's crucial as we begin to uncover more delicate items that could provide invaluable historical insights."

They decided to allocate a portion of their recent funding to acquire these technologies, seeing them as essential investments in the future of their project. The rest of the day was spent planning the integration, discussing potential challenges, and setting a timeline for implementation.

As the sun set over Delphi, the site was quiet but for the soft hum of generators powering their equipment. Nathanial and Dr. Carter looked over the excavation area, their faces lit by the glow of their laptops, discussing the future.

"These tools aren't just new gadgets; they're gateways to deeper understanding," Nathanial mused, closing his laptop with a sense of accomplishment.

Dr. Carter smiled, her eyes reflecting a similar excitement. "Exactly. And with these, we're not just preserving the past; we're ensuring it continues to inform and enrich the future."

The day closed on a note of optimistic anticipation, with Nathanial and Dr. Carter confident that the new tools would not only enhance their current project but also set a new standard for archaeological research worldwide.

With the symposium behind them and new technologies at their disposal, Nathanial Dove and Dr. Helen Carter shifted their focus to the next phase of their project at Delphi: planning a comprehensive exhibition. This exhibition was intended not only to showcase their findings but also to educate the public about the significance of their discoveries and the sophisticated astronomical knowledge of the ancient Greeks.

In their temporary office filled with excavation charts, artifact photos, and research notes, Nathanial and Dr. Carter met with their team, including museum curators and exhibition designers, to discuss the layout and thematic structure of the exhibition.

"Good morning, everyone," Nathanial started, spreading out a digital map of the exhibition space on the screen. "Our goal is to create an immersive experience that not only displays the artifacts but also tells the story of Delphi and its celestial significance."

Dr. Carter took over, pointing to the different sections of the map. "We're planning several key areas. The first section will introduce Delphi's history and its role in the ancient world. From there, visitors will move to a second area focused on the tools and methods used in our excavations."

One of the museum curators, Maria, chimed in, "I suggest we use interactive displays for that part. Perhaps touch screens where visitors can simulate the excavation process or view 3D reconstructions of the site at various stages."

"That's a great idea, Maria," Dr. Carter agreed. "Interactive elements will make the exhibition more engaging, especially for younger visitors. We also want to include a section dedicated to the celestial map and its interpretations."

Nathanial nodded, "Exactly, Helen. And for the celestial map, I think an animated projection could be effective. It could show how the alignments change over time and how they correlate with our findings."

The exhibition designer, Lucas, who had been taking notes, spoke up. "For the artifact display, we can use ambient lighting to highlight the textures and inscriptions. It'll enhance the visitors' ability to see the details that are often missed in typical museum lighting."

Dr. Carter smiled, pleased with the suggestion. "Ambient lighting sounds perfect, Lucas. We also need to ensure that the descriptions are accessible, not just filled with academic jargon. They should tell the story, explain the significance of each item in layman's terms."

As they moved through the planning process, Andreas, responsible for security, raised a point of concern. "Given the value and fragility of these artifacts, we'll need robust security measures throughout the exhibition. Not just surveillance, but also cases that can protect the artifacts from environmental damage and potential tampering."

"Absolutely, Andreas," Nathanial responded. "Let's coordinate with the security technology providers to integrate state-of-the-art systems. Safety of the artifacts is our priority."

The team spent the rest of the day finalizing the themes, selecting artifacts for display, and discussing the catalog that would accompany the exhibition. They planned a soft opening for local schools and historians before the public launch, aiming to gather feedback and make any necessary adjustments.

As the meeting wrapped up, Nathanial looked around at the team, feeling a surge of pride and excitement. "This exhibition is going to be more than just a display; it's going to be an educational journey. Thank you all for your hard work and creative ideas."

Dr. Carter added, "This is the culmination of years of dedication. It's our chance to bring the history of Delphi to life for everyone who visits."

The planning session ended with a sense of accomplishment. Everyone involved was motivated by the challenge of making ancient history resonate with modern audiences, bridging the gap between past and present with innovative displays and storytelling. As they left the meeting, the team was energized, ready to turn their plans into reality, ensuring that the exhibition would be a highlight in the cultural calendar and a fitting tribute to the mysteries of Delphi.

Chapter 14
The Cult's Hidden Base

In the aftermath of the symposium and amidst the preparations for the upcoming exhibition, a new lead emerged that would once again shift the focus of Nathanial Dove and Dr. Helen Carter. Andreas, the head of security, brought to their attention some suspicious activities that had been observed on the outskirts of Delphi, hinting at the possible location of Dr. Moros's group, which had been quietly amassing more followers and resources.

Inside their makeshift office at the dig site, Andreas briefed Nathanial and Dr. Carter on his findings. "I've been monitoring the communications and movements of some of the fringe groups we discussed before. It seems there's a pattern that suggests they might be converging near the old quarry outside of town. It's isolated, and there have been reports of unusual activities at night."

Nathanial looked concerned. "Do we think this is related to Moros and his followers?"

"It's a strong possibility," Andreas replied. "The descriptions of the vehicles and some of the individuals match those seen at the symposium. They could be setting up a more permanent base there."

Dr. Carter, ever cautious, added, "We need to verify this information before jumping to any conclusions. It's crucial we understand what they're planning, especially if it could threaten the site or our work."

Nathanial nodded in agreement. "Andreas, can you arrange for discreet surveillance of the area? Perhaps some night vision cameras or even a drone sweep. We need eyes on that location without raising any alarms."

"Already on it," Andreas confirmed. "I'll handle it personally. We should have some initial footage and data by tomorrow."

The conversation shifted to how they would handle the situation if the suspicions were confirmed. "If Moros is indeed setting up a base there, it could be for a number of reasons," Nathanial speculated. "They might be planning more rituals, or worse, looking to seize artifacts or influence the site directly."

Dr. Carter, thinking ahead, suggested, "We might also need to inform local authorities at some point, but only after we're certain. Any false alarms could backfire, especially with the exhibition coming up."

"That's a good point, Helen," Nathanial agreed. "Let's keep this information tight for now. Only the three of us and a select few from the security team should be aware until we know more."

As they wrapped up their meeting, the weight of the new lead lingered in the air. The possibility of confronting Moros's group more directly was a daunting prospect, but Nathanial and Dr. Carter were determined to protect their findings and ensure the safety of their team.

Later that evening, as Nathanial reviewed the site maps and the locations in relation to the quarry, Dr. Carter joined him, her expression one of resolve. "Nathanial, whatever comes of this, we need to be prepared for possible confrontation. Moros hasn't been overtly hostile yet, but we can't assume that will remain the case."

"You're right," Nathanial acknowledged, looking up from the maps. "We'll take every precaution. Our first priority is the safety of our team and securing the artifacts. Anything that threatens that needs to be handled swiftly and decisively."

With a plan in place to gather more information, they both felt slightly more in control of the situation. Still, the uncertainty of what might be found at the quarry cast a shadow over their usual end-of-day routines. As they left the office, the fading light over Delphi seemed to mirror their mood—hopeful yet cautious, ready to face whatever challenges the new lead might bring.

Under the cover of night, Andreas led a small, select team equipped with night vision goggles and infrared cameras towards the old quarry on the outskirts of Delphi. The moon cast a faint light over the rugged landscape, aiding their stealthy approach. Every member of the team was acutely aware of the stakes involved—not just the potential discovery of Dr. Moros's operations but also the need to maintain complete secrecy.

As they neared the quarry, Andreas signaled for the team to hold their positions while he scouted ahead. The quarry, abandoned for decades, provided numerous hiding spots and shadows under which illicit activities could go unnoticed.

Andreas returned shortly, his expression tense but controlled. "There are definitely people there, and it looks like they've set up some sort of camp. I saw at least a dozen tents and some equipment that could be used for excavations—or something else."

Back at the makeshift command center set up in a van parked a safe distance away, Nathanial listened intently over the radio as Andreas described the scene. Dr. Carter, who had insisted on being part of the operation, sat beside him, her focus sharp.

"Can you tell if they have any security measures in place?" Nathanial asked through the radio, his voice low.

"Not obvious ones," Andreas replied. "But I'm going to circle around the back to get a better look. I'll keep low and slow."

As Andreas and his team moved cautiously, they deployed small, remote cameras that sent live feeds back to the van. The screens flickered with images of the quarry, revealing more details of the encampment. There were crates that seemed out of place for a simple camping trip, and some of the equipment looked decidedly high-tech.

Dr. Carter leaned closer to one of the screens, squinting. "Look there, those crates—are those symbols what I think they are?"

Nathanial adjusted the focus. "They look like antiquities markings. This could be serious. They might be planning to smuggle artifacts."

The gravity of the situation settled over them as they watched the feeds. It was one thing to suspect foul play, but quite another to see potential evidence of it.

After completing his reconnaissance, Andreas returned to the van. "It's as we feared. They've got a setup that suggests they're not just here for some benign purpose. I found traces of recent digging, and those crates definitely look like they're for transporting artifacts."

"What's our next move?" Dr. Carter asked, her mind racing through the legal and ethical implications.

"We need to inform the authorities," Nathanial decided, his tone resolute. "But we have to do it carefully. We can't tip them off, or they might move everything before any action can be taken."

Andreas nodded in agreement. "I suggest we keep a watch overnight and call the police in at dawn. We'll give them the exact coordinates and everything we've observed."

"Let's set up shifts to keep watch," Dr. Carter suggested. "We can't afford to let this site out of our sight until the authorities take over."

The rest of the night was spent in vigilant monitoring, with each team member taking turns to watch the live feeds. The quiet darkness of the area was a stark contrast to the tense anticipation within the van.

As dawn approached, with the first light casting long shadows over the landscape, Nathanial made the call to the local police, providing them with detailed information about the situation. The response was swift, with assurances of immediate action.

Sitting back, Nathanial and Dr. Carter exchanged a weary but determined look. "Once this is over, we'll need to reassess our security measures," Nathanial said, the weight of leadership heavy on his shoulders.

Dr. Carter nodded. "And perhaps push for more stringent regulations on archaeological sites nationwide. This could be a turning point."

As the first police vehicles appeared on the horizon, heading towards the quarry, Nathanial and Dr. Carter prepared to assist in any way they could, ready to protect Delphi's heritage at all costs.

As dawn broke over the old quarry outside Delphi, the police, along with Nathanial Dove and Dr. Helen Carter, descended upon the site. The early morning light revealed the extent of the encampment that Dr. Moros and his followers had established. The area was littered with equipment, tents, and several crates that Nathanial and Dr. Carter had seen through the night vision cameras.

The police moved quickly and efficiently, cordoning off the area and beginning their search of the tents and materials found on site. Nathanial and Dr. Carter, along with Andreas, were allowed to accompany the officers as observers, given their vested interest in the outcome.

As they walked through the camp, the scale of Moros's operation became evident. Notebooks, maps, and other documents were strewn about, some containing detailed notes on celestial alignments and others with sketches that looked suspiciously like maps of archaeological sites, including areas of Delphi not yet excavated by any official team.

In one of the larger tents, the police uncovered a makeshift lab setup with equipment that was clearly used for artifact restoration or perhaps modification. Nearby, a table was covered with what appeared to be recently unearthed artifacts, some still caked in dirt, clearly not handled with the care that such ancient items demanded.

Nathanial, examining one of the maps, pointed out to Dr. Carter, "Look at this, Helen. It's a detailed plan of the northern sector of our site. This isn't just a random dig; they knew exactly where they wanted to go."

Dr. Carter, deeply concerned, responded, "This could mean there's a leak somewhere in our team, or at the very least, in the broader archaeological community. We need to tighten our security protocols and perhaps even revisit our vetting processes."

As the police continued their search, they called over Nathanial and Dr. Carter to examine a particularly disturbing find: a small pit where it appeared artifacts had been buried, possibly in an attempt to hide them or maybe even smuggle them out at a later time.

"Seems like they were planning to come back for these," one of the officers noted, pulling out a statuette that might have been part of a larger ceremonial piece.

The implications were serious, and Nathanial felt a surge of responsibility to ensure these artifacts were preserved and studied properly. "We'll need to document everything here and then arrange for these items to be transported to the museum under guard," he said, his voice firm.

Dr. Carter nodded, adding, "And I'll start drafting a report on this incident for the archaeological record. It's crucial that we keep transparent records of these events to help prevent anything similar in the future."

As the operation wound down, the police confirmed that they had detained several individuals, including Dr. Moros, who were found hiding near the back of the quarry. The evidence collected suggested that this group had been involved in unauthorized excavations and possibly the sale of artifacts on the black market.

With the site secured and the sun fully risen, Nathanial, Dr. Carter, and Andreas headed back to their base at Delphi. The morning's events had cast a new light on the challenges they faced, not just in terms of excavation and preservation, but also in protecting their sites from those who would exploit them.

The drive back was quiet, each lost in their thoughts about the implications of the morning's discoveries. They knew the road ahead would be challenging, requiring not only scientific acumen but also a strategic approach to safeguarding their work. The day had begun with a covert operation, but it had opened up a broader battle against the theft and exploitation of cultural heritage—a battle they were now fully committed to fighting.

As the police finished processing the scene at the quarry and began transporting the detained individuals and recovered artifacts, Nathanial Dove, Dr. Helen Carter, and Andreas discussed the implications of the day's events on their return to the Delphi site. The atmosphere was tense, with each aware of how closely they had skirted a significant threat to their project.

"That was too close for comfort," Andreas remarked as he drove. "It's unsettling to think about how much damage they could have done if they had more time."

Dr. Carter nodded in agreement, her voice reflecting her concern. "Yes, and it's alarming to consider that there might be more groups like Moros's out there. We need to reevaluate our site security and possibly our collaboration protocols."

Nathanial, looking out the window, deep in thought, finally spoke. "We also need to consider the possibility of an inside leak. It's too coincidental that Moros knew exactly where to dig. We might need to tighten our information security, maybe even conduct some background checks on the team."

Dr. Carter sighed, "That's going to create a lot of extra work and potentially some trust issues within the team. But you're right, Nathanial. We can't afford another breach."

Andreas added, "I'll coordinate with the local police to keep a watch on the site for the next few weeks, just in case there are any other groups watching us or Moros tries to send someone else after his things."

As they approached the Delphi site, Nathanial's phone rang. It was the police chief, updating him on the situation. "Dr. Dove, just to let you know, we've had a bit of a situation here. One of Moros's associates tried to escape during transport. We caught him, but it was close. He was desperate, almost violent."

Nathanial's grip on his phone tightened. "Thank you for the update, Chief. This confirms that we're dealing with more than just amateur archaeologists. Please keep us informed of any other developments."

Hanging up, he relayed the news to Dr. Carter and Andreas. "This is far from over. Moros's people are not just enthusiasts; they're potentially dangerous. We might be dealing with a network, which means we have to stay vigilant."

Dr. Carter nodded gravely. "Let's arrange a team meeting first thing tomorrow. We need to brief everyone and make sure they understand the seriousness of this situation. Everyone needs to be extra cautious, especially when off-site."

Andreas, pulling into the site parking area, chimed in. "I'll set up temporary security checkpoints at all access points. No one gets in or out without a thorough check. It's going to be tight, but better safe than sorry."

As they disembarked from the vehicle, the weight of their responsibilities pressed heavily upon them. The quiet of the site offered a stark contrast to the turmoil of the day, and as they walked towards their offices, each felt the burden of the decisions that lay ahead.

"That was a narrow escape, indeed," Nathanial mused aloud. "But it's also a wake-up call. We've been focused so much on the historical battles these artifacts represent that we almost missed the modern battle being waged right under our noses."

Dr. Carter agreed, "It's a reminder that the past isn't just something to be studied—it's something that continues to have power and relevance. We need to be as strategic in our planning and protection as we are in our excavations."

With the moon casting long shadows across the excavation site, the team felt the echo of the ancient past mingling with the urgency of the present. Tomorrow's meeting would be critical in redefining their approach to safeguarding their work, their team, and the invaluable heritage of Delphi.

Chapter 15
The Power of Belief

In the calm after the storm of recent events, Nathanial Dove and Dr. Helen Carter found themselves in the tranquil setting of the Delphi archaeological site, reflecting on their encounter with Dr. Moros and his followers. The early morning air was crisp, and the site was bathed in the soft light of dawn, providing a serene backdrop for their conversation.

Nathanial broke the silence, his voice contemplative. "Helen, what do you think motivated Moros and his group? It was more than just curiosity. There was a fervor there, almost a desperation."

Dr. Carter considered his words, looking out over the ruins. "I think it's a powerful reminder of how belief can drive people. Moros believed so strongly that there was hidden knowledge or power here that it justified all his actions, however misguided."

Nathanial nodded slowly. "Yes, the power of belief. It can inspire great things, but it can also lead people astray. We saw that firsthand. It's a fine line between passion and obsession."

Dr. Carter sighed. "Exactly. And as researchers, we walk that line constantly. We have our beliefs, our theories, but we must constantly check them against the evidence, remain open to being wrong. That's the key difference between us and Moros."

Nathanial picked up a small stone from the ground, turning it over in his hand. "This whole ordeal has made me think about our responsibilities as stewards of history. We have the power to shape how these ancient stories are told and understood. It's a heavy responsibility."

Dr. Carter looked at him, her expression earnest. "It is. And it's why we need to be vigilant, not just about external threats like Moros but also about how we handle the information we uncover. How we interpret and share it can have big implications."

Nathanial replaced the stone gently on the ground. "I've been thinking about that a lot lately. About our role in this bigger historical narrative. We need to ensure that our work does not just add to the knowledge base but also respects the cultures and peoples we study."

Dr. Carter nodded in agreement. "Our work has to bridge cultures, time, and ideologies. It's about creating understanding, not division. What happened with Moros... it's a reminder of what happens when beliefs become rigid and unyielding."

Nathanial looked across the site, the first rays of the sun illuminating the ancient stones. "How do we ensure we remain open, Helen? How do we safeguard against becoming so convinced of our theories that we close off other possibilities?"

Dr. Carter smiled slightly, her gaze thoughtful. "Continuous questioning, Nathanial. We must question our findings, our interpretations, ourselves. And we must encourage our peers to question us too. Science, at its best, is a dialogue, an ongoing conversation."

Nathanial nodded, absorbing her words. "A dialogue... yes, that's a good way to put it. And perhaps that's what was missing with Moros. There was no dialogue, just a monologue."

Dr. Carter agreed. "Exactly. And moving forward, we need to foster more dialogue, both within the academic community and with the public. Our exhibitions, our presentations—they're all opportunities to engage in that conversation."

As they prepared to leave the site for the morning, Nathanial turned to Dr. Carter. "Today, I feel more committed than ever to that dialogue, Helen. Let's ensure our work at Delphi continues to invite conversation, challenge assumptions, and inspire both awe and understanding."

Dr. Carter nodded, her spirit renewed by their reflection and the peaceful surroundings. "Let's do exactly that, Nathanial. Let's use our research to build bridges, not walls."

With a renewed sense of purpose, they walked back towards their offices, ready to continue their work, guided by the lessons learned from their recent encounters. The challenges were many, but so were the opportunities—to learn, to share, and to connect the past with the present in meaningful ways.

In the days following their reflective discussion, Nathanial Dove and Dr. Helen Carter poured their renewed commitment and insights into finalizing the plans for the upcoming exhibition. They gathered with their team in the main conference room, surrounded by layouts and digital mockups displayed on large screens.

"Okay, team, let's focus on integrating our recent findings into the exhibition narrative," Nathanial began, pointing to a section of the digital layout on the screen. "We need to ensure that each display not only informs but also engages and challenges our visitors."

Dr. Carter took over, her enthusiasm evident. "We've discussed adding a section that directly addresses the complexity of interpreting archaeological data. I think this could be a key part of our narrative, showing how different beliefs and biases can influence interpretations."

Maria, the exhibition designer, nodded and responded, "I've drafted some ideas for interactive displays that could allow visitors to explore this concept. For instance, we could have a digital touchscreen where visitors can see how changing certain variables like date ranges or artifact placement could alter the entire understanding of an excavation site."

"That sounds fantastic, Maria," Dr. Carter approved. "It would really underscore the point that archaeology isn't just about digging up artifacts, but about piecing together narratives from the past, which can vary widely depending on perspective."

Lucas, responsible for multimedia integrations, chimed in. "We could also use augmented reality to show how different theories would have changed the physical layout of ancient Delphi. Visitors could 'see' the site change through different historical interpretations."

Nathanial smiled, pleased with the team's creativity. "These are great ideas. Let's make sure we also highlight the role of technology in modern archaeology. We want to demonstrate how advancements like 3D scanning and infrared imaging have transformed our field, making it possible to validate or challenge long-held beliefs."

Dr. Carter added, "And let's not forget about the importance of preserving these findings. Perhaps a section dedicated to conservation techniques, showing before and after images of artifacts that were preserved using the new methods we've adopted."

As the meeting continued, the team discussed logistical aspects of the exhibition, such as the flow of visitor traffic, which artifacts would be replicas for hands-on exploration, and which would be behind protective glass.

"Regarding the artifact security," Andreas interjected, "we need to be absolutely sure that our most valuable pieces are secure. I suggest we implement an advanced surveillance system around the high-value displays."

Nathanial nodded in agreement. "Security is paramount. We've seen what can happen when valuable artifacts are not adequately protected. Andreas, work with Lucas to integrate security measures that are effective yet unobtrusive."

As the session wrapped up, Nathanial addressed the team with a sense of pride. "Everyone, this exhibition isn't just a display of what we've found. It's a narrative about the journey of discovery, the challenges we face, and the evolving nature of knowledge. It's about inspiring our visitors to think critically about history and how it's told."

Dr. Carter concluded, "And it's a testament to the power of belief—not just in terms of what we're willing to accept as true but in our belief in the value of seeking, learning, and understanding. Let's make sure that comes through in every aspect of this exhibition."

With their plans more refined and their objectives clear, the team felt energized. The exhibition at Delphi was shaping up to be not just an educational event, but a transformative experience for all who would visit.

As the preparations for the exhibition at Delphi entered their final stages, Nathanial Dove and Dr. Helen Carter prepared to address the media. The buzz surrounding their recent findings and the upcoming exhibition had attracted considerable attention, not just from the academic community but also from the public and the press. Given the controversies that had shadowed their recent symposium, both knew the importance of clear and effective communication.

On the morning of the press conference, the ancient site of Delphi served as a dramatic backdrop. Camera crews and journalists from various international media outlets had set up their equipment, capturing the picturesque views of the ruins that stretched out behind the podium.

Nathanial stood at the podium, his presence calm and authoritative as he began to speak. "Good morning, and thank you for joining us today at this site of historical and cultural significance. We are here to share not only our recent archaeological findings but also to introduce our forthcoming exhibition, which aims to provide a deeper understanding of Delphi's past through both scientific and cultural lenses."

Dr. Carter followed, addressing the specific aspects of the exhibition. "Our exhibition, 'Delphi: Echoes of the Past,' will showcase a series of interactive displays and carefully preserved artifacts that bring to life the rich history of this site. It's designed to engage visitors of all ages in the ongoing dialogue between the past and present."

Journalists raised questions about the nature of the recent findings and their implications. One reporter asked, "Could you elaborate on how these new findings might change our understanding of ancient Delphi?"

Nathanial responded, "Certainly. Our recent excavations have uncovered artifacts and structural remains that suggest Delphi was a hub of not only religious and cultural activities but also of scientific endeavor, particularly in the field of astronomy. These findings provide compelling evidence of the advanced observational capabilities of the ancient Greeks."

Another journalist inquired about the controversy at the symposium related to the interpretation of these findings. "How do you respond to the criticisms regarding the interpretation of archaeological evidence, especially in light of the disputes at the symposium?"

Dr. Carter took this question, her tone reassuring yet firm. "Archaeology, like any science, is continually evolving. We base our interpretations on a rigorous examination of evidence, and we remain open to revising those interpretations as new evidence comes to light. The debates at the symposium reflect a healthy scientific process where differing viewpoints are expressed and examined."

As the conference drew to a close, Nathanial emphasized the educational goals of the exhibition. "We hope that this exhibition will inspire visitors to appreciate the complexities of archaeological research and the insights it can provide into human history. We invite everyone to explore the connections between the past and their own lives, fostering a deeper appreciation for the legacy of places like Delphi."

After the press conference, Nathanial and Dr. Carter felt a sense of accomplishment. They had addressed the media's questions with transparency and had highlighted the scientific and educational values of their work, reinforcing the importance of maintaining an open dialogue about the past.

The rest of the day was spent in final preparations for the exhibition opening. As they walked through the exhibition space, checking each display, Nathanial remarked, "Handling the media well is just as important as the excavations themselves. It's about crafting the narrative that reaches the public."

Dr. Carter nodded, looking around at the nearly completed exhibition. "And tomorrow, we open this narrative to the world. Let's hope it resonates as strongly with our visitors as it has with us."

Confident in their preparations and the power of the work they were about to present, they left the site at dusk, the ancient stones of Delphi casting long shadows behind them, silent witnesses to the new chapter they were about to unveil.

The day after the press conference, as final touches were being applied to the exhibition, Nathanial Dove received an unexpected communication from Marcus Levant, an old colleague and one-time rival who had kept a keen eye on the developments at Delphi. The message requested a meeting, and Nathanial, curious and somewhat cautious, agreed to meet Marcus at a small café near the site.

As Nathanial sat waiting, Marcus approached, his demeanor one of polite professionalism mixed with a hint of the competitive edge that had always characterized their interactions. "Nathanial, it's been too long," Marcus greeted him, extending his hand, which Nathanial shook firmly.

"Indeed, it has, Marcus. I was surprised to hear from you," Nathanial replied, motioning for Marcus to sit. "What brings you to Delphi?"

Marcus took a seat, his eyes scanning the area before focusing back on Nathanial. "I've been following your work, and the recent discoveries. It's impressive, though I must admit, the controversies at the symposium caught my attention."

Nathanial nodded, expecting this might be the direction of their conversation. "Yes, those were unfortunate but perhaps inevitable given the nature of our findings. We're pushing boundaries, and that often invites debate."

Marcus leaned forward slightly, his interest apparent. "True. And it's your handling of these debates that interests me. You've managed to maintain a balanced approach, promoting open dialogue while standing firm on your scientific principles. It's admirable."

"Thank you, Marcus. We strive to be thorough and open in our research. Speaking of which, how have your own projects been?" Nathanial asked, steering the conversation to include Marcus's pursuits.

Marcus smiled, a twinge of pride in his expression. "Busy as ever. But let's not deflect too much. I'm here because I think there's potential for collaboration between your team and mine. Our focus on the ritualistic aspects of ancient sites could complement your astronomical and archaeological work."

Nathanial considered this, intrigued despite his natural caution. "I'm open to discussing that, Marcus. Collaboration could indeed enrich both our projects. What did you have in mind?"

"Perhaps a joint research initiative," Marcus suggested. "Combining our resources and expertise could lead to a more comprehensive understanding of these sites. My team could provide insights into the cultural and religious contexts, while yours could continue to unearth the physical and astronomical elements."

"That sounds promising," Nathanial acknowledged. "But given the sensitivity of our recent work, any collaboration would need to be approached carefully. We need to ensure that our research integrity remains intact."

"Of course," Marcus agreed. "I propose we start with a small pilot project. Something that allows both teams to gauge the dynamics of a collaboration without committing to anything too large-scale."

Nathanial nodded, seeing the wisdom in a cautious approach. "A pilot project could work. Let's draft some proposals and see where our interests best align. We'll also need to discuss how findings are communicated, to avoid any potential public misunderstandings."

"Agreed," Marcus said, his tone earnest. "Nathanial, I believe this could be the beginning of something very beneficial, not just for our teams, but for the broader academic community."

As they parted ways, with plans to meet again soon to formalize their collaboration, Nathanial felt a cautious optimism. Working with Marcus could indeed open new avenues of research and provide fresh perspectives on the ancient mysteries of Delphi.

Reflecting on the conversation as he walked back to the site, Nathanial was reminded of the power of belief—not just in the supernatural or the mystical, but in the potential for change, growth, and new understanding through the collaboration of diverse minds. As he looked over the preparations for the exhibition, he felt more convinced than ever of the path they were on, ready to embrace whatever new challenges and opportunities it might bring.

Chapter 16
The Final Stand

The day of the exhibition opening at Delphi arrived with a mix of anticipation and excitement. Nathanial Dove and Dr. Helen Carter arrived early in the morning to oversee the final preparations. The exhibition, titled "Delphi: Echoes of the Past," was set to unveil their recent archaeological findings to the public, complete with interactive displays and meticulously preserved artifacts that told the story of ancient Delphi and its astronomical significance.

As the sun rose over the site, casting a golden glow on the ancient stones, the team was busy with last-minute adjustments. The exhibition spaces were filled with the hum of activity as multimedia installations were tested, lighting adjusted, and security protocols double-checked.

Nathanial walked through the exhibition halls, inspecting each display to ensure that everything was perfect. The sections of the exhibition were thoughtfully laid out to guide visitors through a journey back in time. Starting from the history of Delphi as a cultural and religious center, the path led through intricate displays explaining the excavation methods, findings, and the scientific processes behind their conclusions.

At the heart of the exhibition was the interactive section that Dr. Carter had envisioned. Here, visitors could engage with digital touchscreens that allowed them to explore how different variables, such as date ranges or artifact placement, could alter the understanding of an excavation site. Another feature was the augmented reality setup where visitors could see the site change through different historical interpretations, giving them a sense of walking through time.

Dr. Carter joined Nathanial in the central hall, where a large-scale projection mapped the celestial alignments as they would have appeared over Delphi thousands of years ago. "It looks wonderful, Nathanial," she remarked, her voice filled with pride. "It's exactly how we envisioned it. Engaging, educational, and hopefully, inspiring."

Nathanial nodded, his eyes scanning the room. "It's more than just an exhibition; it's a testament to our team's hard work and dedication. I hope it makes the visitors feel connected to this place and its history."

As the opening hour approached, the staff took their positions, and the first groups of visitors began to arrive. Families, students, historians, and tourists from around the world gathered, their faces bright with curiosity and awe as they stepped into the ancient world of Delphi.

The exhibition began smoothly, with visitors marveling at the artifacts, engaging with the interactive displays, and immersing themselves in the augmented reality experiences. Nathanial and Dr. Carter circulated among the guests, answering questions and discussing their work.

One particularly enthusiastic visitor, a teacher leading a group of high school students, approached Dr. Carter. "This is incredible, Dr. Carter. It makes history come alive for these students in a way that textbooks just can't match."

Dr. Carter smiled, pleased. "That's exactly what we hoped for. We want to ignite a passion for history and archaeology in young minds. It's not just about learning facts; it's about understanding our collective past and its impact on our present."

As the day progressed, the positive reactions from the visitors reinforced the team's confidence in the value of their work. The exhibition was not only a showcase of their findings but also a vibrant educational tool that bridged the gap between ancient history and modern technology.

Nathanial, watching a group of children marvel at a reconstructed ancient artifact, felt a profound sense of accomplishment. "We've done something important here, Helen," he said quietly to Dr. Carter as they observed the crowd. "We've brought Delphi to the world, not just as a site of ruins, but as a living, breathing place of history."

Dr. Carter nodded in agreement, her eyes reflecting the success of the day. "Yes, we have. And this is just the beginning."

As the sun began to set over Delphi, casting long shadows across the exhibition grounds, the site buzzed with the energy of discovery. It was a fitting tribute to the enduring legacy of one of the world's most historic sites, marking a successful opening day that promised many more insights and inspirations to come.

As the first day of the exhibition continued, the buzz and excitement among the visitors remained palpable. It was mid-afternoon when Marcus Levant, whose proposed collaboration with Nathanial and Dr. Carter had recently been discussed, made his appearance at the exhibition. His arrival was not announced, but Nathanial spotted him immediately, navigating through the displays with a keen eye and a notebook in hand.

Nathanial approached him with a welcoming smile. "Marcus, glad you could make it," he said, extending his hand.

Marcus shook it warmly. "Nathanial, I wouldn't miss this. You've done an impressive job here. This exhibition is quite the achievement."

"Thank you, Marcus. I'm eager to hear your thoughts," Nathanial replied, gesturing towards the central hall. "Shall we walk through together? I can give you some insights into our key displays."

"That sounds excellent," Marcus agreed, and they began to walk through the exhibition, starting with the interactive displays that allowed visitors to explore archaeological techniques.

As they approached the augmented reality section, Marcus commented, "This AR setup is fascinating. It visually contextualizes the findings in a way that's quite engaging."

Nathanial nodded, "Yes, we wanted to give visitors a real sense of how Delphi might have looked at different points in history. It's about making the past accessible and relevant."

They continued to the section dedicated to the celestial alignments, where Nathanial explained, "Here we have integrated our latest research on the astronomical significance of Delphi. It's been one of the more challenging aspects of our work, given the complexities of ancient astronomy."

Marcus, looking intrigued, leaned in to examine some of the detailed descriptions next to a digital model. "I see you've used a variety of sources to corroborate these findings. It's meticulous work. How has it been received so far?"

"Quite well, actually," Nathanial responded. "It seems to spark a lot of curiosity about how advanced these ancient civilizations were in their understanding of the cosmos."

As they moved to a quieter part of the exhibition, Marcus's tone became more serious. "Nathanial, about our potential collaboration—I've been giving it a lot of thought. I believe there's a wealth of opportunity for both our teams to benefit from each other's expertise."

Nathanial agreed, "I've been thinking along the same lines, Marcus. I believe your insights into the cultural and religious aspects could greatly enhance our archaeological interpretations."

Marcus stopped walking, turning to face Nathanial directly. "I propose we start with a joint study. Perhaps a paper or a series of workshops? We could combine our data and see where it leads us."

"That sounds like a promising start," Nathanial replied, thoughtful. "A joint paper would allow us to integrate our findings and test how well our teams work together. If successful, it could lead to more permanent collaboration."

Marcus nodded, jotting something down in his notebook. "I'll draft a preliminary proposal then. We could focus on a comparative analysis of the religious practices at Delphi, using both your archaeological data and our ethnographic research."

"Let's do that," Nathanial confirmed. "And let's ensure we keep the lines of communication open. I want this collaboration to be built on transparency and mutual respect."

Marcus smiled, closing his notebook. "Agreed. Nathanial, I'm looking forward to what we can discover together."

As Marcus departed, Nathanial watched him go, feeling cautiously optimistic about their future work together. The exhibition had not only been a celebration of past achievements but also a launching point for new ventures. Nathanial returned to the bustle of the exhibition, ready to handle whatever challenges and opportunities lay ahead.

As the first day of the exhibition drew to a close, the atmosphere at Delphi remained charged with the energy of discovery and scholarly exchange. However, this positive atmosphere was disrupted when a small group of protesters, apparently followers of Dr. Moros who had not been detained, made their way into the exhibition area. Their leader, a tall, charismatic figure who had been seen with Moros at the symposium, began loudly challenging the findings presented in the exhibition.

Nathanial Dove, alerted by one of the security team members, approached the scene with Dr. Helen Carter. They found the protesters gathered around the celestial alignments display, where the leader was vocally criticizing the interpretation of the artifacts.

"This is a misrepresentation of our ancestors' knowledge!" the protester exclaimed, drawing the attention of nearby visitors. "You are diluting the truth with your so-called scientific methods!"

Nathanial stepped forward, his demeanor calm yet firm. "Sir, I understand you have strong feelings about this topic, but we encourage respectful dialogue here. If you have specific concerns, we're happy to discuss them in a more appropriate setting."

The protester turned to face Nathanial directly. "Our concerns are that you ignore alternative interpretations that don't fit your narrow view of science. You dismiss anything that suggests our ancestors had advanced understanding beyond what you deem plausible."

Dr. Carter joined in, her voice steady. "We base our interpretations on rigorous analysis and peer-reviewed research. We are open to discussing differing viewpoints, but we must rely on evidence that can be substantiated."

"Your evidence is selected to support your conclusions!" another protester chimed in, visibly agitated.

Nathanial, maintaining his composure, replied, "Our research is transparent, and our findings are open for review. We invite constructive criticism, but it must be grounded in factual debate, not just contradiction."

The confrontation attracted a crowd of visitors, some curious, others concerned. Security personnel hovered nearby, ready to intervene if necessary.

Seeing that the situation might escalate, Dr. Carter suggested, "Perhaps we can arrange a seminar or a discussion forum where these issues can be debated more thoroughly. It's important that this exhibition remains a place of learning and exchange, not conflict."

The leader of the protesters hesitated, then nodded slowly. "A forum, yes. That could be a place to present our evidence, to show that there are alternative ways to interpret the signs left by our ancestors."

Nathanial agreed, "We'll organize it. Let's continue this discussion in a way that promotes understanding and respect on all sides. For now, I ask that you respect the purpose of this exhibition and allow our visitors to explore it peacefully."

Reluctantly, the protesters agreed to withdraw, and the crowd began to disperse. Nathanial and Dr. Carter exchanged relieved glances, aware that they had managed to defuse a potentially volatile situation.

After the protesters had left, Dr. Carter turned to Nathanial. "We need to be prepared for more challenges like this. The forum will be a good opportunity to address these alternative views openly and to demonstrate the integrity of our research approach."

Nathanial nodded, looking over the now calm exhibition hall. "It's an ongoing challenge, balancing different beliefs and interpretations. But it's essential for the progress of knowledge. We'll plan this forum carefully, make it a constructive dialogue."

As they walked back to their offices, both felt the weight of their responsibilities not just to the past, but to fostering an environment where history could be explored from multiple angles, always with respect and a commitment to truth. The day had ended on a tense note, but it reinforced their resolve to continue their work with openness and rigor.

In the days following the public confrontation at the exhibition, Nathanial Dove and Dr. Helen Carter worked diligently to organize the promised forum. They intended it to be a platform for open dialogue where various interpretations of the archaeological findings could be discussed. They hoped that by engaging directly with critics and the public, they could foster a deeper understanding and possibly turn the tide of skepticism and controversy into a more constructive discourse.

The forum was set to take place in a large tent set up specifically for this purpose, adjacent to the main exhibition area. Chairs were arranged in a semi-circle to encourage a sense of inclusivity and openness. A panel was assembled, including Nathanial, Dr. Carter, a couple of their team members, and, surprisingly, two of the more articulate members of the group that had protested, including their leader, who had agreed to participate constructively.

As the attendees began to fill the tent, the atmosphere was charged with a mix of anticipation and apprehension. Nathanial opened the forum with a brief introduction. "Thank you all for joining us today. This forum is a testament to our commitment to open scholarly dialogue. We believe that by discussing our differences and challenges openly, we can all gain a deeper understanding of the complex histories we are trying to uncover and interpret."

The leader of the protesters, introduced as John, took his turn to speak. "We appreciate this opportunity. It's important that all voices are heard, especially those that challenge mainstream interpretations. Our perspective is that the conventional archaeological community often overlooks or dismisses evidence that could suggest more advanced ancient technologies or understandings."

Dr. Carter responded thoughtfully, "We recognize that our interpretations are based on the best evidence available and that this evidence can be interpreted in multiple ways. However, our approach is always grounded in scientific methodology, which requires verifiable data."

The discussion moved into specific examples, with John citing instances he believed showed bias or oversight in archaeological interpretations. Nathanial and Dr. Carter countered with explanations of their methodologies, often turning the debate back to the importance of peer-reviewed research and evidential support.

One audience member, a local teacher, asked, "How do we teach our students about these debates without confusing them about what to believe?"

Dr. Carter smiled, appreciative of the question. "That's an excellent point. We should teach them not just facts but how to think critically about information. Show them how to weigh evidence, consider different viewpoints, and understand the basis of scientific inquiry. It's about asking the right questions, not just knowing the right answers."

As the forum continued, the tone gradually shifted from confrontational to more conversational. Participants began to see the value in each other's viewpoints, recognizing that while they might not agree on all points, they shared a common goal of understanding the past.

John, in a closing remark, conceded, "While I may not agree with every interpretation presented by your team, I respect the rigor of your approach. Perhaps there is more room for us to contribute to this process, to ensure that various hypotheses are considered."

Nathanial concluded the forum with reflective optimism. "Today has shown that dialogue is not only possible but essential. Let's continue this conversation, not as adversaries but as collaborators in the pursuit of knowledge. We may discover that our perspectives are not as divergent as they seem."

As the attendees dispersed, many stayed to discuss informally, exchanging ideas and contact information. The forum had not resolved all differences, but it had opened a pathway for more respectful and productive discussions.

Dr. Carter, walking back to the exhibition with Nathanial, felt a sense of accomplishment. "I think we've turned a corner today, Nathanial. It's a small step, but it's in the right direction."

Nathanial agreed, looking back at the tent now emptying of people but filled with lingering discussions. "Yes, we've started something important here. Let's keep the momentum going."

The day had indeed marked a turning point, not just in addressing the immediate controversies but in setting a new standard for how such debates could be conducted in the future.

As the exhibition at Delphi drew to a close, Nathanial Dove and Dr. Helen Carter took time to reflect on the events of the past weeks. The forum had set a new tone of openness and dialogue that resonated not just within their team but also among the public and the previously skeptical groups. Now, as they walked through the quiet exhibition space, they discussed the impact of these efforts and the future steps they would take to foster continued dialogue and collaboration.

Nathanial looked around at the emptying display halls, a sense of fulfillment mixed with relief evident in his demeanor. "Helen, I think we've managed to not only address the immediate issues but also to lay a foundation for ongoing communication. It's been an intense process, but incredibly worthwhile."

Dr. Carter nodded, her eyes scanning the thoughtful notes and feedback left by visitors. "Absolutely, Nathanial. The level of engagement we've seen, especially after the forum, has been remarkable. People are genuinely interested in understanding the complexities of what we do, and they appreciate the transparency."

As they continued their walk, Andreas joined them, his usual stern expression softened by a slight smile. "I've just had a conversation with local authorities and some of the community leaders. They're very pleased with how we handled the situation with the protesters. It seems we've earned some additional support for our future projects here."

"That's excellent news, Andreas," Nathanial responded, his relief apparent. "It's important that we maintain good relationships with the local community. They are, after all, the stewards of this heritage as much as we are."

Dr. Carter, picking up a leftover exhibition pamphlet, added, "I think our next step should be to organize a series of workshops. Maybe some focused on the local schools to get young people excited about archaeology and history. It could be a way to extend the educational impact of what we've started here."

Nathanial considered this, nodding thoughtfully. "Yes, let's do that. Education is key. The more we engage with the younger generation, the better we can ensure the preservation of sites like Delphi. Plus, it might inspire future archaeologists."

They spent a few moments in silence, each lost in thoughts of future plans and the potential to expand their outreach. Finally, Dr. Carter spoke up, "We should also consider how we can use what we've learned from this exhibition and forum to improve how we handle public engagements and controversies in future projects."

"Agreed," said Nathanial. "I'll draft a proposal for a new community engagement strategy. It seems the more we involve the public in our work, the more supportive they become. We need to build on that."

As the day ended, and the last of the visitors departed, Nathanial, Dr. Carter, and Andreas stood together, looking out over the site. The shadows grew longer, and the setting sun cast a golden hue over the ancient stones.

"It's been quite a journey," Nathanial said quietly, a reflective tone in his voice. "But I feel like today marks a new beginning, not just an end."

Dr. Carter smiled, her eyes reflecting the sunset. "A new beginning indeed. Let's keep pushing forward, learning, and growing. Not just as researchers, but as communicators and educators."

With the exhibition officially over, they each felt a sense of accomplishment and anticipation for the future. The challenges they had faced had strengthened their resolve and deepened their commitment to their work and to each other.

As they left the site, the air was cool and the sky a deepening blue. Delphi, with its ancient mysteries and timeless presence, remained a powerful reminder of the enduring pursuit of knowledge and understanding—a pursuit that Nathanial, Dr. Carter, and their team were more dedicated to than ever.

Chapter 17
The Calamity Averted

After the successful conclusion of the exhibition at Delphi, Nathanial Dove and Dr. Helen Carter took a moment to reflect on their achievements and the challenges they had overcome. They sat together in the quiet of Nathanial's office, surrounded by notes and artifacts that told stories of ancient civilizations, now more accessible thanks to their efforts.

Nathanial leaned back in his chair, his eyes thoughtful. "We've come a long way, Helen. From the initial discoveries to the controversies and the exhibition—it's been quite the journey."

Dr. Carter nodded, her expression one of quiet satisfaction. "Indeed, it has. I think we've managed not just to avert a potential calamity but also to advance the public's understanding of what we do. The engagement at the exhibition was beyond what I had hoped."

Nathanial smiled, picking up a small artifact from his desk—a ceramic shard with inscriptions that had been one of the highlights of the exhibition. "This piece sparked so many conversations. It's incredible to think about how these ancient objects continue to speak to us, isn't it?"

"It is," Dr. Carter agreed, watching the light play over the shard. "And speaking of conversations, the forum we organized was a pivotal moment. It turned the tide in how people viewed our work and the challenges we face in interpreting the past."

Nathanial placed the shard down gently. "The forum was a risk, but it paid off. Engaging directly with skeptics and those with alternative views helped demystify our processes and intentions."

The room was filled with a comfortable silence as they both pondered the recent events. Then, Dr. Carter spoke up again, "One thing I've been thinking about is how we can apply the lessons we've learned here to future projects. The proactive approach to public engagement, the forums, the educational outreach—it could redefine how archaeological projects are conducted globally."

Nathanial looked intrigued. "That's an excellent point. Perhaps we could draft a white paper on our experiences here. It could serve as a case study for both the archaeological community and other fields where public scrutiny and participation are increasing."

"That's a brilliant idea," Dr. Carter responded with enthusiasm. "A white paper would not only document our experiences but also offer a roadmap for others. It could discuss everything from crisis management and public relations to educational strategies and community involvement."

Nathanial nodded, already making mental notes. "Let's allocate some time next week to outline the key components of the paper. We could include sections on methodology, public engagement, dealing with controversies, and the integration of technology in archaeological research."

Dr. Carter agreed, adding, "And let's not forget the impact of teamwork. This project would not have been possible without the dedication and diverse skills of our entire team. Highlighting the importance of collaboration across different expertise could be an invaluable part of the paper."

As their discussion drew to a close, Nathanial and Dr. Carter felt a renewed sense of purpose. The challenges they had faced at Delphi had not only tested their resolve but had also deepened their understanding of the broader implications of their work.

Nathanial stood up, stretching slightly. "Well, Helen, let's get started on that paper soon. There's a lot to cover, and I think it could really make a difference."

Dr. Carter stood as well, ready to head out. "Absolutely, Nathanial. Let's do it. This could be just as important as any of our finds in the field."

They left the office together, stepping out into the fading light of the day, their minds alive with possibilities and plans for the future. The project at Delphi had been a turning point, not just for them but potentially for the field of archaeology as a whole. As they walked, they discussed potential titles for their white paper, both aware that the next chapter of their professional journey was just beginning.

In the weeks following the closure of the Delphi exhibition, Nathanial Dove and Dr. Helen Carter initiated a thorough monitoring process to assess the long-term impacts of their public engagement strategies and the overall exhibition. They were particularly interested in understanding how their efforts influenced public perceptions of archaeology and the preservation of cultural heritage.

One sunny afternoon, they convened in Nathanial's office, surrounded by feedback forms, digital analytics from the exhibition's app, and a collection of emails from educators and cultural organizations expressing interest in their work.

Nathanial, reviewing a graph on his laptop, shared some initial findings. "It looks like our visitor numbers exceeded expectations, and the feedback on the interactive displays has been overwhelmingly positive. People appreciated the chance to engage directly with the archaeological process."

Dr. Carter, sifting through a stack of feedback forms, nodded. "Yes, and there's a recurring theme here about how the exhibition changed visitors' perceptions. Many noted that they hadn't realized how detailed and scientific archaeology is, or how it can illuminate aspects of ancient cultures in such a dynamic way."

Nathanial looked pleased. "That's exactly what we were hoping for. We wanted to demystify our field and open it up to public scrutiny and understanding. It seems we've made some headway."

The discussion then shifted to the educational impact, particularly on local schools. Dr. Carter held up a letter from a local high school teacher. "This teacher wants to develop a curriculum module based on our exhibition. They're asking for our input on resources and potential guest lectures."

"That's fantastic," Nathanial responded enthusiastically. "Supporting education like this could be a vital part of our outreach. Let's set up a meeting with this teacher and maybe others who are interested. We could create a comprehensive package that schools can use, not just locally but eventually nationally."

As they discussed the educational outreach, Andreas entered the room, bringing in a new set of data about online engagement. "The virtual tour and webinars we set up have had significant traction, especially from international visitors who couldn't travel to the exhibition. The analytics show a lot of engagement from North America and Europe, and surprisingly strong numbers from Asia."

Nathanial considered this. "We should think about how we can maintain and possibly expand this digital engagement. Perhaps ongoing webinars or a virtual lecture series could be effective."

Dr. Carter agreed, adding, "And let's not forget about the potential for collaboration with other archaeological sites around the world. Sharing insights, methodologies, and public engagement strategies could strengthen global efforts in cultural preservation."

The team spent the rest of the afternoon strategizing how to leverage the success of the exhibition into long-term benefits for the field of archaeology. They planned further analysis of visitor data to refine their outreach strategies and discussed developing professional development workshops for educators.

As they wrapped up their meeting, Nathanial reflected on the progress they had made. "This project has grown beyond our initial expectations. We're not just conducting research; we're actively participating in the cultural dialogue of our times."

Dr. Carter, packing up her documents, smiled in agreement. "It's a big responsibility, but it's also a great opportunity. We're helping shape how the public understands and values the past."

With a plan to monitor the ongoing effects of their work and adapt their strategies as needed, Nathanial and Dr. Carter left the office feeling optimistic. They were making a tangible impact, not just in uncovering history, but in ensuring it played a meaningful role in contemporary society. The lessons learned from Delphi were proving invaluable, guiding them as they continued to navigate the complexities of their field.

Several months after the successful exhibition at Delphi, Nathanial Dove and Dr. Helen Carter were invited to speak at an international conference on cultural heritage and archaeology. The event was held in a large conference hall filled with scholars, researchers, and students from around the globe, all eager to hear about the innovative approaches Nathanial and Dr. Carter had implemented at Delphi.

As they prepared for their presentation in the green room, Dr. Carter looked over their slides. "Nathanial, do you think we've emphasized enough about the community involvement aspect? It was a major factor in our success."

Nathanial, reviewing his notes, nodded. "I think we have, but let's make sure to highlight it during the Q&A session. The community's role in archaeological projects is often underestimated, and our experience at Delphi proves how vital it is."

They walked onto the stage to a warm reception. Nathanial started the presentation by discussing the challenges they had faced at the beginning of their project, particularly the public's skepticism and the controversy surrounding their findings.

"As many of you know, engaging the public in our archaeological work isn't just about opening up dig sites for tours. It's about integrating the public's perspective into our research, ensuring that our work not only uncovers history but also resonates with contemporary audiences," Nathanial explained.

Dr. Carter then took over, focusing on the strategies they used to turn these challenges into a dynamic dialogue. "We initiated several programs aimed at demystifying archaeological processes. This included interactive exhibitions, forums for public debate, and extensive educational outreach. These initiatives helped us bridge the gap between our work and the public's interest."

A slide showed photos of visitors at the exhibition, particularly children, using the interactive displays. "These hands-on experiences were particularly effective. They not only educated the visitors but also sparked a deeper curiosity about archaeology and ancient history."

The presentation then shifted to the tangible outcomes of their engagement efforts. Dr. Carter detailed, "Post-exhibition surveys showed a significant increase in local and international interest in Delphi's heritage. This has not only boosted tourism but has also increased funding for further research and preservation efforts."

During the Q&A session, a scholar from Brazil asked, "Could you elaborate on how you handled the integration of potentially conflicting interpretations of your findings, especially with groups like those led by Dr. Moros?"

Nathanial answered, "That was one of our toughest challenges. We remained committed to transparency and scientific rigor, offering forums for all viewpoints to be expressed and discussed. It was crucial that these discussions were framed respectfully and informatively, which helped in alleviating tensions and fostering a more inclusive understanding of our work."

Another question came from a student interested in the technical aspects: "What role did technology play in engaging the public and in your research?"

Dr. Carter responded, "Technology was pivotal. From augmented reality that visualized ancient Delphi through different historical periods to digital kiosks that allowed deeper exploration of artifacts, technology enabled us to present our findings in more engaging and accessible ways."

As the session concluded, the feedback was overwhelmingly positive. Many attendees expressed admiration for the Delphi project's innovative approach to public engagement and were eager to implement similar strategies in their own work.

Nathanial and Dr. Carter left the stage feeling validated and inspired. Their work had not only impacted Delphi but was now influencing the broader field of archaeology, promoting a more interactive and inclusive approach to studying and preserving the past.

Backstage, they discussed plans to compile their methods and findings into a comprehensive guide for other professionals. "This could be our next big project, Helen," Nathanial suggested.

Dr. Carter smiled in agreement. "Absolutely, Nathanial. Let's turn our experience into a resource that can help transform how archaeology interacts with the world."

As they mingled with other scholars and attendees, their conversation turned to future projects and collaborations, each discussion reinforcing the broader impact of their work at Delphi—a testament to the power of integrating community, technology, and open dialogue in the preservation and interpretation of cultural heritage.

As the international conference concluded, Nathanial Dove and Dr. Helen Carter took a moment to reflect on their journey since the Delphi project began. They sat in a quiet corner of the conference hall, the bustle of departing attendees creating a backdrop of murmured conversations and the shuffling of papers.

"It's incredible to think about where we started with this project, isn't it?" Nathanial mused, his gaze thoughtful. "From those first digs to the controversies and the exhibition... It's been quite the expedition, not just professionally but personally as well."

Dr. Carter nodded, a reflective smile crossing her features. "Absolutely. I feel like we've both grown tremendously through these challenges. We've learned not just about archaeology, but about leadership, resilience, and the importance of community engagement."

Nathanial looked at her, his expression earnest. "And about collaboration. Working so closely with you, learning from your approach to problem-solving and engagement—it's changed the way I think about leadership in our field."

Dr. Carter's smile widened. "Thank you, Nathanial. I could say the same about you. Your dedication to maintaining scientific integrity while being open to public dialogue has taught me a lot about balancing different aspects of our profession."

They both took a moment to enjoy the quiet reflection, appreciating the mutual respect and camaraderie that had developed between them. It was this partnership that had steered their project through its many trials and led to its successes.

"As we look to the future," Nathanial continued, "I think the lessons we've learned here will shape our next projects. Not just the archaeological work, but how we approach our roles as educators and community figures."

Dr. Carter nodded, her mind already turning to future possibilities. "Indeed. And speaking of the future, I've been offered a position to lead a new cultural heritage initiative. It's a significant opportunity to apply what we've learned on a larger scale."

Nathanial's eyes lit up with interest. "That sounds like an amazing opportunity, Helen. Congratulations! I can't think of anyone better suited to it."

Dr. Carter chuckled lightly. "Thanks, Nathanial. I'm excited about it. And what about you? Any new horizons on your path?"

Nathanial paused, considering his next steps. "I've been thinking about a project that combines archaeological research with global educational programs. The idea is to not only discover but to share those discoveries in ways that directly benefit educational communities worldwide."

"That sounds like a wonderful initiative," Dr. Carter responded, genuinely impressed. "Using archaeology to enhance education across borders—it's ambitious and so needed."

As their conversation wound down, they stood up, ready to leave the conference behind and step into the next phases of their careers. "Helen, working with you on the Delphi project has been one of the highlights of my career. I'm looking forward to seeing all the incredible work you'll do in your new role," Nathanial said, offering his hand.

Dr. Carter shook his hand warmly. "And I'm equally excited to see where your new project leads you, Nathanial. Let's keep in touch, and who knows? Perhaps our paths will cross again on some future dig or conference."

With a final exchange of good wishes, Nathanial and Dr. Carter parted ways, each stepping into a new chapter filled with potential and promise, carrying with them the lessons and successes of their time at Delphi. The challenges they had faced together had not only fortified their professional resolve but had also enriched their personal growth, leaving them better equipped for whatever lay ahead.

In the quiet aftermath of the conference, as Nathanial Dove walked back to his hotel, the cool evening air gave him a moment to contemplate the future. His mind buzzed with ideas and plans, a testament to the stimulating discussions and new connections he had made over the past few days. The success at Delphi had opened new doors, and now he faced the exciting prospect of steering his career in a direction that could potentially redefine his role as an archaeologist and educator.

Back in his hotel room, Nathanial sat at the desk, a notebook open in front of him, as he sketched out the preliminary concepts for his new project. The idea was to create a series of global educational programs linked directly to live archaeological sites, using virtual reality and online platforms to bring real-time discoveries into classrooms around the world.

As he outlined the objectives and potential partnerships, his phone rang. It was Dr. Carter, and her voice was full of the same energy and enthusiasm she always brought to their collaborations.

"Nathanial, I've been thinking about our conversation earlier. Your project could really use a strong educational component on cultural heritage and conservation. Have you thought about integrating that angle more deeply?"

Nathanial smiled, grateful for her insight. "I was just working on that, actually. I think there's tremendous potential to not only teach about archaeology but also to instill a sense of global stewardship for cultural heritage. I'd love to get your thoughts on some of the educational modules I'm considering."

"I'd be happy to help," Dr. Carter replied. "And Nathanial, I've spoken with a few contacts who might be interested in funding a pilot program. They're very keen on projects that combine technology and education."

"That's fantastic, Helen," Nathanial said, his enthusiasm growing. "Let's set up a time to draft a proposal. I think with your connections and the preliminary data we have from Delphi, we could really make a compelling case."

"Agreed," Dr. Carter said. "And Nathanial, I think it's important that we continue to involve local communities in this project, much like we did in Delphi. Their insights and participation could enrich the program immensely."

"Absolutely," Nathanial responded. "Their involvement is essential. It's about building a global community of learning and preservation."

As they finalized their plans to collaborate on the proposal, Nathanial felt a profound sense of anticipation for what the future held. After they hung up, he stood at the window, looking out over the city lights, pondering the impact their work could have not just on students and academics but on broader public awareness and involvement in archaeology.

The next morning, Nathanial met with several potential collaborators to discuss the technological aspects of his project. The meetings were productive, and each conversation opened up more possibilities, from using satellite imagery to enhance site analysis to developing an app that could allow users to explore archaeological sites in augmented reality.

Filled with a sense of purpose and direction, Nathanial spent the evening drafting the first version of his project proposal. Each sentence he wrote was imbued with the lessons learned from Delphi—the importance of dialogue, the value of public engagement, and the profound impact of integrating education with archaeological discovery.

As Nathanial prepared to leave the conference and return home, he was not just returning with plans for future projects but with a renewed vision for his role as an archaeologist. He was more determined than ever to make archaeology accessible and engaging to people from all walks of life, bridging the gap between past and present, and between cultures across the globe. The challenges of Delphi had prepared him well for this mission, and he looked forward to the adventures and opportunities that lay ahead.

Chapter 18
New Beginnings

Nathanial Dove's vision for integrating archaeological discoveries with global educational outreach was taking a concrete shape. After several months of planning, securing funding, and building partnerships, he was ready to launch the Dove Foundation for Archaeological Research and Education. The foundation aimed to connect students and educators worldwide with archaeological sites through cutting-edge technology and in-depth educational programs.

On the morning of the launch, Nathanial stood in the newly renovated headquarters of the foundation, a spacious building equipped with state-of-the-art facilities, including a virtual reality lab, a conference center for workshops, and a live feed studio that could broadcast directly from archaeological sites. The walls were adorned with photos and artifacts from various digs, each telling a story of historical discovery.

Today's event was the culmination of all these efforts, marked by an inaugural symposium titled "Bridging Past and Present: The Role of Archaeology in Modern Education." Distinguished guests from around the world, including educators, technologists, historians, and archaeologists, were invited to attend.

As guests began to arrive, Nathanial reviewed the agenda with his team. The symposium would feature panels on the importance of preserving cultural heritage, the integration of technology in archaeology, and strategies for engaging young people with history in meaningful ways.

The opening ceremony started with Nathanial addressing the audience, sharing his vision for the foundation. "Today marks the beginning of a new chapter in how we connect with our past," he announced. "The Dove Foundation is committed to fostering an appreciation for archaeology across global communities and inspiring future generations to preserve and understand their cultural heritage."

Following Nathanial's speech, the first panel discussion explored innovative methods of teaching history through interactive technology. Experts demonstrated how virtual reality could transport students to ancient civilizations, allowing them to explore historical sites and artifacts in ways that books and photos could never achieve.

In the VR lab, a group of invited students experienced their first virtual dig, guided by Nathanial's team. They were equipped with VR headsets and controllers that allowed them to "excavate" a digital reconstruction of an archaeological site Nathanial had previously worked on. Their excitement and curiosity filled the room, a tangible testament to the foundation's potential impact.

Meanwhile, the live feed studio was officially inaugurated with a broadcast from a dig site in Egypt, where one of Nathanial's colleagues led a live tour, explaining their recent findings to the symposium attendees. This session not only showcased the technological capabilities of the foundation but also emphasized its global reach and collaborative spirit.

Throughout the day, Nathanial met with various stakeholders to discuss potential collaborations. These conversations often centered around expanding the foundation's resources to include more archaeological sites and developing a curriculum that could be integrated into school systems worldwide.

The event closed with a commitment from several educational institutions to incorporate the foundation's resources into their teaching modules. Nathanial also announced a series of upcoming workshops designed for educators to learn how to use archaeological resources in their classrooms effectively.

As the guests departed, Nathanial and his team gathered to debrief. The launch had been a resounding success, exceeding their expectations in both turnout and enthusiasm. The positive feedback from the panel discussions and the interactive sessions confirmed that there was a significant interest and need for the foundation's offerings.

With the foundation now officially launched, Nathanial felt a profound sense of accomplishment and anticipation. He knew that the road ahead would be filled with challenges, but also incredible opportunities to change how people viewed and learned about history. As the team left the building, the lights of the foundation's sign flickered on, casting a warm glow over the entrance. It was a symbol of hope and progress, a beacon for future explorations and discoveries that would bridge past and present for generations to come.

Following the successful launch of the Dove Foundation for Archaeological Research and Education, Nathanial Dove convened a strategic planning meeting with his core team. The purpose was to set a detailed agenda for the foundation's first year of operations, focusing on project timelines, educational outreach, and technological developments.

The meeting took place in the foundation's conference room, where Nathanial and his team gathered around a large table strewn with laptops, documents, and digital tablets.

"Alright, team, let's start with our primary objectives for the year," Nathanial began, projecting a digital agenda on the screen at the front of the room. "Our main goal is to expand our reach into schools globally and to deepen our research initiatives at key archaeological sites. I want to ensure that every project we undertake aligns with our mission to educate and engage."

Dr. Helen Carter, now leading the educational outreach program, took the lead on the first item. "For our educational outreach, I propose we start with a pilot program involving schools in three different regions: North America, Europe, and Asia. We'll use our virtual reality platforms to bring the archaeological sites directly into classrooms, allowing students to explore and learn in a dynamic environment."

Nathanial nodded in approval. "Helen, that sounds excellent. How do you plan to measure the success of these pilot programs?"

"We'll use a combination of pre- and post-engagement surveys, performance on module assessments, and teacher feedback to gauge the effectiveness of the content and the technology," Helen explained. "This data will help us refine the programs before a wider roll-out."

Next, the discussion moved to technological development, led by Marcus, the head of the technology team. "We're developing a new version of the VR platform that includes interactive tools for students to conduct virtual digs. They'll be able to uncover artifacts, catalog them, and learn about their historical context right within the VR environment."

Nathanial was particularly interested in this development. "Marcus, ensure that the interface is user-friendly for younger students but also has advanced features for our university-level participants. Can we integrate AI to guide the students through the digs?"

"Yes, we're planning to include an AI assistant that can provide information and prompts based on the user's actions in the VR environment. It's quite cutting-edge and should make the learning experience both informative and engaging," Marcus replied.

The meeting then addressed the research initiatives. Dr. Carter suggested, "Given our successful dig at Delphi, I think we should consider expanding our presence there and possibly exploring new sites that have potential for similar discoveries. Collaboration with local universities and research institutions will be key."

Nathanial agreed, "Absolutely, Helen. Let's draft some proposals for potential partnership projects. Also, we should consider hosting a series of symposia on site, inviting international researchers to join us. It would boost our profile and foster collaborative research."

As the meeting drew to a close, Nathanial summarized the discussion. "It seems we have a solid plan moving forward. Helen, Marcus, I trust you to oversee the implementation of these programs and keep me updated on your progress. We need to ensure that everything we do upholds the standards of excellence we're committed to."

"Absolutely, Nathanial," Helen responded, her determination evident. "This is an ambitious agenda, but we have the right team and the right vision."

Nathanial concluded, "Thank you, everyone. Let's make this first year a foundation we can build on for the future. Our goal is not just to educate but to inspire a new generation of archaeologists and historians."

With a clear agenda set, the team felt energized and ready to tackle the ambitious projects ahead. As they left the conference room, there was a shared sense of purpose and excitement about the impact their work could have on the world of archaeology and beyond.

Two months into the launch of the Dove Foundation, Dr. Helen Carter was spearheading the educational initiatives, a core aspect of the foundation's mission. She arranged a series of meetings with educators, curriculum developers, and technology experts to refine and expand the educational programs that the foundation offered. One key meeting included a virtual session with educational partners from various international schools.

As the meeting commenced, Dr. Carter greeted the participants warmly. "Thank you all for joining today. This session is crucial as we shape the educational components of our programs. Our goal is to ensure that our modules are not only engaging but also academically robust and culturally sensitive."

A curriculum developer from a partner school in Singapore shared her screen, displaying a draft of the curriculum module. "We've integrated the virtual excavation tools into the science curriculum, which allows students to explore archaeological methods as part of their studies on earth sciences and history."

Dr. Carter nodded approvingly. "That's a fantastic integration. How have the students responded to the pilot tests?"

"The feedback has been overwhelmingly positive," the developer replied. "Students enjoy the hands-on aspect, and it seems to help them grasp complex concepts more easily. However, we need to ensure the historical content is accurate and up-to-date, which is where your team's expertise is invaluable."

Dr. Carter responded, "Absolutely, we will provide continuous updates and training for teachers. We're also developing a series of webinars that delve deeper into the archaeological background of the sites featured in the VR modules. This should help teachers feel more confident in facilitating these sessions."

Another participant, a technology integration specialist from a school in Germany, raised a question. "Regarding the VR platform, are there specific hardware requirements? Some of our schools have limited tech resources, and we need to ensure the program is accessible."

Marcus, who was also attending the meeting, took this question. "We've designed the VR platform to be as accessible as possible. It can run on basic VR setups that are becoming increasingly common in schools. Additionally, we're exploring options for a non-VR version that can run on standard computers or tablets."

Dr. Carter added, "Accessibility is key for us. We want this program to reach as many students as possible, regardless of their school's technology budget. Marcus, perhaps we could also look into a grant program that could help under-resourced schools acquire the necessary equipment."

"That's a great idea, Helen. I'll start putting together a proposal for potential funding sources for such grants," Marcus confirmed.

The conversation shifted to the content of the modules. An educator from the UK discussed the need for culturally diverse perspectives in the historical narratives provided in the modules. "It's important that the content is not only engaging but also representative of diverse archaeological perspectives, especially when discussing regions with rich cultural histories like the Middle East or South America."

Dr. Carter acknowledged this point. "You're absolutely right. We're committed to presenting balanced perspectives and including local archaeological experts in the content creation process. It's essential that the histories and cultures we're teaching about are represented by those who are also part of them."

As the meeting wrapped up, Dr. Carter summarized the action items. "Thank you, everyone, for your invaluable input today. We will revise the curriculum modules based on this discussion, enhance the technological accessibility of our platforms, and seek funding for the grant program to support schools. Let's reconvene in a month to review progress and tackle any new challenges that have emerged."

With clear objectives set and the collaboration of international educational partners, the Dove Foundation's educational initiatives were well on their way to making a significant impact. Dr. Carter felt a deep sense of fulfillment as she ended the call, knowing that their efforts were paving the way for a new generation to explore and appreciate the complexities of human history through the lens of archaeology.

As the Dove Foundation's initiatives began to gain traction globally, it became apparent to Nathanial Dove that the team needed to expand to meet the increasing demands and opportunities. He scheduled a meeting with Dr. Helen Carter and Marcus, the technology lead, to discuss recruitment strategies and identify key areas where additional expertise was necessary.

The trio gathered in a small conference room, each equipped with a laptop and notes. Nathanial initiated the discussion, projecting a digital chart showing the foundation's current projects and their staffing needs.

"Looking at our current projects and future commitments, it's clear we need to bring more people on board," Nathanial began. "We need expertise not only in archaeology and education but also in areas like digital content creation, project management, and possibly more specialized technical roles for our VR and AR developments."

Dr. Carter nodded in agreement, her eyes scanning the chart. "I agree, Nathanial. Especially with the educational programs expanding, we need more curriculum developers and possibly educators with experience in interactive and digital learning environments."

Marcus chimed in, focusing on the technical aspects. "On the technology side, we could really use some additional software developers, especially those with experience in VR and AR platforms. Also, considering the data we're managing, a data analyst could help us make sense of user interactions and feedback to improve our offerings."

Nathanial took notes as they spoke, outlining the job roles that needed to be filled. "Let's prioritize these roles then. Helen, could you take the lead on recruiting for the educational positions? And Marcus, would you manage the tech recruitments?"

Dr. Carter quickly drafted some notes on her laptop. "Absolutely, I'll start drafting job descriptions for the educational roles. I think reaching out to our academic networks and possibly advertising in educational technology forums would be a good start."

Marcus was already browsing his contacts list. "I have a few leads on potential candidates for the tech roles. I'll reach out personally to gauge interest and then follow up with formal job postings. I'll focus on platforms that cater to tech professionals with VR and AR experience."

Nathanial looked pleased. "Excellent. And I think it's crucial we emphasize the foundation's mission in these job postings. We want team members who are not only skilled but also passionate about using their talents to bridge past and present through education and technology."

Dr. Carter, always keen on maintaining a cohesive team culture, added, "I'll also set up a series of team integration workshops. As the team grows, it's important that everyone is aligned with our mission and feels part of our community."

"That's a great idea, Helen. Ensuring the new hires blend well with our culture is as important as their technical skills and experience," Nathanial agreed.

As they wrapped up the meeting, Marcus suggested, "Should we also consider internships? It could be a good way to bring in fresh ideas and foster talent among students who are currently studying relevant fields."

Nathanial considered this for a moment, then nodded. "Let's explore that too. Interns can bring in new perspectives, and it's a great way for us to give back to the academic community by providing practical experiences."

With a clear plan in place, the meeting concluded with each member of the team understanding their responsibilities in the recruitment process. They were excited about the prospect of new talents joining the foundation, contributing to its diverse projects, and helping achieve its ambitious goals.

As Nathanial left the conference room, he felt confident about the foundation's future. With a strong team in place, they could continue to innovate and expand their impact on archaeological education and public engagement globally.

As the year drew to a close, Nathanial Dove and Dr. Helen Carter decided to convene a year-end review with their team at the Dove Foundation.

The meeting, held in the foundation's main conference room, was both a reflection on the year's successes and challenges, and an opportunity to discuss the goals for the coming year.

Nathanial opened the meeting with a brief speech. "This year has been a foundational one for the Dove Foundation. Thanks to everyone's hard work and dedication, we've not only launched significant projects but also expanded our team and our reach. Today, let's review what we've accomplished and outline our priorities for the next year."

Dr. Carter then took the floor to discuss the educational initiatives. "Our educational programs have been a resounding success. We've integrated our curriculum into over 100 schools worldwide and our virtual reality platform has been especially popular among students. However, there's always room for improvement. We need to focus on gathering more detailed feedback to better understand the impact of our programs."

Nathanial nodded in agreement. "Feedback is crucial. It informs our strategies and helps us make informed decisions. Marcus, how's the tech side doing in terms of development and user feedback?"

Marcus responded, "We've made significant improvements to the VR platform, especially in making it more user-friendly. The next step is to implement AI-driven analytics to track user engagement and learning outcomes more precisely. This will allow us to customize and improve the learning experience based on real-time data."

"That sounds promising," Nathanial said. "Helen, perhaps we can integrate this data-driven approach into our educational content as well?"

"Absolutely," Dr. Carter replied. "Using data to tailor our educational offerings will make them more effective and engaging. It's about evolving with our audience's needs."

The discussion then shifted towards the new recruits. Nathanial asked, "How are the new team members settling in? Are there any challenges we need to address?"

Dr. Carter took a moment before answering. "The integration has gone smoothly for the most part. But as we continue to grow, maintaining our foundation culture and mission becomes more challenging. We might need to think about more structured onboarding processes and perhaps regular team-building activities."

"That's a good point," Nathanial acknowledged. "Let's plan to develop a comprehensive onboarding program early next year. It's important that everyone not only understands their role but also feels a part of our community."

As the meeting drew to a close, Nathanial encouraged everyone to share their personal reflections on the year and their aspirations for the future. One by one, team members discussed what they had learned, the challenges they had faced, and what they hoped to achieve moving forward.

Finally, Nathanial concluded the meeting. "Looking forward, let's keep pushing the boundaries of what we can achieve. Next year, we'll not only expand our existing projects but also explore new opportunities for growth. Let's continue to be leaders in using archaeology to educate and inspire."

As everyone left the conference room, there was a shared sense of accomplishment and excitement for the future. The foundation had not only survived its initial year but thrived, laying down a solid groundwork for further success. Dr. Carter and Nathanial lingered for a moment, reflecting on the journey.

"We've built something great here, Helen," Nathanial said, a hint of pride in his voice.

"We really have," Dr. Carter agreed, smiling. "And the best part is, we're just getting started."

With the new year on the horizon, they were ready to take on whatever challenges and opportunities it might bring, driven by a shared commitment to making history accessible and engaging to people around the world.

Chapter 19
Reflections

In the quiet solitude of his office, Nathanial Dove found himself reflecting on the transformative journey of the Dove Foundation. The walls, lined with artifacts and photos from various digs, served as a testament to the adventures and discoveries that had marked his career. Now, with the foundation thriving, he pondered the broader implications of their work, particularly the role of perspective in understanding and interpreting the past.

Nathanial's thoughts were interrupted by a gentle knock on the door. Dr. Helen Carter entered, holding a stack of educational materials that had been developed as part of the foundation's outreach. "Nathanial, I've been reviewing our curriculum updates and thinking about how much our perspective shapes our teaching. It's fascinating how different interpretations can coexist, each adding layers to our understanding."

Nathanial nodded, gesturing for her to sit. "Absolutely, Helen. It's something I've been thinking about a lot lately. The power of perspective not only shapes our understanding of history but also how we present that history to others. It's about more than just facts; it's about narratives, and every narrative is influenced by the perspective of its teller."

Dr. Carter laid the materials on his desk. "I think that's why our approach has been so well-received. We don't just teach facts; we explore the implications of those facts from various angles. It challenges students to think critically, not just about history, but about how history is constructed."

Nathanial leaned back in his chair, considering this. "That's a crucial point, Helen. Our work doesn't exist in a vacuum. The context in which we present historical data can influence public perception just as much as the data itself. This is particularly true when dealing with contentious or complex historical periods."

The discussion turned to a recent feedback session they had conducted with educators using their curriculum. "One teacher mentioned that her students were particularly engaged when they could see how historical interpretation has evolved over time," Dr. Carter continued. "It seems that understanding that history is not static— that it evolves with new findings and changing societal values—really resonated with them."

"That's an insightful observation," Nathanial responded. "It underlines the importance of teaching history as a dynamic discipline. Perhaps we need to emphasize this more explicitly in our programs. It's not just about learning what happened in the past, but also about understanding how our perceptions of those events have changed—and continue to change."

As they delved deeper into the philosophy behind their educational approach, Nathanial thought about the various archaeological projects the foundation was involved in. Each project, from the deserts of Egypt to the jungles of Central America, offered not only new insights into ancient civilizations but also new perspectives on how those civilizations interacted with their environments and each other.

"These projects," Nathanial mused aloud, "they're not just about unearthing artifacts. They're about uncovering stories. And each story is colored by the lenses through which we view them. Our job is to provide as clear a lens as possible."

Dr. Carter smiled, picking up the curriculum notes again. "And to provide as many different lenses as possible, too. Each perspective offers a unique insight, and together, they provide a fuller picture."

As the meeting concluded, Nathanial felt invigorated by their discussion. It reinforced the importance of the foundation's work and the responsibility they carried. He watched as Dr. Carter left the office, the stack of materials in her hands a small but significant part of their efforts to educate and enlighten.

Returning to his reflections, Nathanial was reminded of the ever-evolving nature of knowledge. Each discovery, each story, and each perspective added to the rich tapestry of human history. And as they continued to teach, learn, and discover, they contributed not just to historical knowledge, but to a deeper understanding of what it means to view the past through many eyes. This understanding, he realized, was perhaps one of the most powerful tools they could offer to the world.

Several weeks after their reflective discussion, Nathanial and Dr. Helen Carter decided to evaluate the impact of the Dove Foundation's initiatives on local and global communities. They organized a community feedback session, inviting participants from the areas where their educational programs had been implemented, as well as representatives from the archaeological sites involved in their projects.

The session was held in a large, sunlit room at the foundation's headquarters, arranged to foster an open and inclusive atmosphere. Around the room, displays showed interactive maps and photos from various projects, each pinpointing a different part of the globe where their work had touched lives.

As people began to gather, Nathanial opened the session with a few words. "Thank you all for joining us today. This feedback is invaluable as it helps us understand the real-world impact of our work. We're eager to hear your thoughts on how our projects have affected your communities and how we might improve our initiatives."

A schoolteacher from a local Delphi school was the first to speak. "Your programs have really ignited a passion for history among my students. They see these ancient sites not just as old rocks but as living stories. However, we struggle sometimes with the technical aspects, especially the VR setups."

Nathanial nodded, making notes. "Thank you for that feedback. We'll look into providing more technical support and perhaps simpler interfaces for younger students. Helen, maybe we could develop some training sessions for teachers?"

Dr. Carter responded immediately, "Absolutely, Nathanial. It's essential that educators feel confident using the tools we provide. We could host workshops right here and create online tutorials."

A representative from a community near an archaeological site in Egypt shared his perspective next. "Your projects have brought a lot of attention to our area, which has been great for tourism. But there's also a concern about the preservation of the site with increased foot traffic."

Nathanial took this seriously. "That's a valid concern. We must ensure that our work benefits communities without harming the cultural heritage we aim to preserve. Perhaps we could collaborate on developing visitor guidelines and enhance our site preservation efforts."

Dr. Carter added, "We could also increase our community outreach to educate visitors about the significance of preservation. Engaging them in protecting these sites could be a way to extend the educational aspect of our work."

The conversation continued with various stakeholders sharing their experiences and suggestions. A university professor from Japan discussed the academic collaborations that had been fostered through the foundation's efforts. "The cross-disciplinary studies you've sponsored are groundbreaking. They have encouraged a more holistic approach to history and culture which has enriched our academic programs immensely."

Nathanial was pleased. "That's wonderful to hear. We hope to expand those academic partnerships. Perhaps we could co-host an international conference on interdisciplinary studies."

As the session drew to a close, Nathanial and Dr. Carter thanked everyone for their candidness and constructive suggestions. They stayed behind to discuss the next steps.

"Helen, today's feedback has been incredibly helpful," Nathanial remarked. "It's clear we're making a difference, but there's still much to do, especially in terms of making our technology more accessible and enhancing site preservation."

Dr. Carter nodded, her mind already racing with ideas. "Let's prioritize these issues. I'll start drafting a plan for the educational support improvements, and we can both work on a proposal for the preservation protocols."

Their discussion was a blend of planning and reflection, acknowledging the strides they had made and the paths still to be charted. As they left the meeting room, both felt a renewed commitment to their mission, bolstered by the community's feedback and inspired by the collaborative potential that lay ahead. The foundation's impact was growing, not just in educational fields but as a catalyst for community development and cultural preservation.

Several months later, Nathanial Dove organized a virtual roundtable to assess the global reach of the Dove Foundation's programs and to brainstorm ways to further expand their impact. Participants included educators, archaeologists, and cultural leaders from various continents, all connected via a sophisticated online conferencing platform that allowed for real-time translation and interaction.

As the session began, Nathanial welcomed the participants with a brief introduction. "Thank you all for joining today. This roundtable is a cornerstone of our commitment to foster global dialogue and cooperation. I'm eager to hear how our programs have been received in your respective regions and discuss how we can enhance our collaborations."

A professor from Brazil was the first to share his thoughts. "Nathanial, your foundation's resources have been instrumental in my courses on South American archaeology. The virtual digs and interactive modules have brought a new level of engagement to my classes. However, we face challenges with internet reliability, which sometimes hinders our ability to fully utilize your tools."

Nathanial responded thoughtfully, "That's a crucial point. We are exploring partnerships with technology companies to enhance internet accessibility in regions facing such challenges. Ensuring reliable access is fundamental to the success of our programs."

Next, a cultural leader from Kenya shared her perspective. "Your efforts to include diverse cultural narratives in your materials have been well-received here. It's vital for our communities to see their histories represented accurately and engagingly. Perhaps further localized content could be developed, reflecting more regional histories and languages."

"That's an excellent suggestion," Dr. Helen Carter, who was also part of the roundtable, chimed in. "We've started working on more localized modules but expanding this effort could indeed deepen our impact. Nathanial, maybe we could set up a dedicated team to focus on regional customization?"

Nathanial nodded in agreement. "Absolutely, Helen. Building a team dedicated to localization will help us be more responsive to the needs of different communities. We'll take that forward."

An educator from Japan raised another point. "The interactive nature of your programs is fantastic, but we also find a strong demand for expert-led sessions where students can interact live with archaeologists. Could there be a way to schedule more live Q&A sessions with your experts?"

"We've seen great interest in those live sessions as well," Nathanial acknowledged. "Let's look at scaling up our live interactions, perhaps by establishing a regular schedule of webinars and Q&A sessions that rotate through various time zones to cover global needs."

As the discussion continued, a university lecturer from France highlighted the importance of follow-up. "While the initial engagement is high with your programs, sustaining that interest is often a challenge. Continuous updates and follow-ups could help maintain the momentum."

Dr. Carter noted this feedback. "Continuity is key. We could develop a series of follow-up modules that build on the initial experiences. Perhaps incorporating ongoing projects and new discoveries could keep the content dynamic and engaging."

The roundtable concluded with a consensus on several strategic enhancements to the foundation's programs. Nathanial thanked everyone for their valuable insights. "This has been an incredibly fruitful discussion. We are committed to incorporating your feedback to expand and improve our outreach. Together, we can continue to make archaeology accessible and relevant across the globe."

After the meeting, Nathanial and Dr. Carter stayed online to outline the action items discussed. "Helen, let's prioritize the enhancement of technological access and the development of localized content. I believe these are critical to our next phase of growth."

Dr. Carter agreed, already drafting a plan. "I'll start outlining proposals for both and coordinate with our tech and educational teams. We have a lot of work ahead, but it's exciting to see the potential unfold."

As they ended their session, both felt a renewed sense of purpose. The global reach of their work was not just about spreading knowledge but about creating a worldwide community connected by a shared interest in preserving and understanding humanity's collective past. The path ahead was clear, and they were ready to meet its challenges head-on.

Nathanial Dove spent the weeks following the global roundtable immersed in planning the future projects of the Dove Foundation. The feedback had been enlightening, pushing him to think broadly about how the foundation could not only expand its reach but also deepen its impact. He sat in his office surrounded by maps, project proposals, and digital screens displaying interactive data from their current programs. It was here that he began to outline the ambitious plans for the upcoming years.

The foundation had identified two major initiatives that would require careful planning and significant resources. The first was the Global Heritage Initiative, which aimed to partner with local communities around archaeological sites to ensure that these projects were beneficial to both the scientific community and the local populace. This initiative would focus on sustainable archaeology, education, and the economic development of the local areas.

The second major initiative was the Virtual Archaeology Network, an expansive digital platform that would host virtual tours, educational modules, and live interactive sessions with archaeologists from various dig sites around the world. This network would also serve as a hub for a series of online courses and workshops aimed at students, educators, and enthusiasts.

Nathanial met with Dr. Helen Carter to discuss these projects in detail. "Helen, these initiatives have the potential to redefine how we engage with archaeology and heritage preservation on a global scale," Nathanial said, his voice filled with enthusiasm.

Dr. Carter, equally excited, responded, "I agree, Nathanial. The Global Heritage Initiative, in particular, aligns perfectly with our mission to make archaeology beneficial and accessible. It's about time we bridge the gap between excavation and community benefit."

As Nathanial and Dr. Carter delved deeper into the planning, they discussed the logistical challenges and potential partnerships that would be crucial for the success of these projects. They decided to collaborate with universities, tech companies, and local governments to gather the necessary resources and expertise.

The Virtual Archaeology Network required careful thought about user interface, accessibility, and educational content. "We need to ensure that the platform is intuitive and engaging for users of all ages and backgrounds," Nathanial noted, as he sketched a rough design of the user interface. "It should feel as if they are stepping onto an archaeological site from their living rooms or classrooms."

For the Global Heritage Initiative, Dr. Carter suggested setting up pilot projects in two different regions to test their approaches before a full rollout. "We should start with a small-scale implementation to iron out any issues and ensure that our model is truly beneficial to the local communities," she advised.

Nathanial agreed, "That's a prudent approach. Let's select the sites carefully, considering both the archaeological potential and the community's needs and interests."

As the meeting concluded, Nathanial felt a mixture of anticipation and responsibility. These projects were not just expansions of the Dove Foundation's work; they were steps towards realizing a vision of archaeology that was participatory, educational, and globally interconnected.

Over the next few weeks, Nathanial and Dr. Carter worked tirelessly with their team, detailing every aspect of the new initiatives from technological needs, educational content, community engagement strategies, to funding models. Each element was meticulously planned to ensure that once launched, the projects would run smoothly and achieve their intended impact.

As the plans for the Global Heritage Initiative and the Virtual Archaeology Network began to take shape, Nathanial often found himself reflecting on the journey that had led him here. From his early days of fieldwork to founding the Dove Foundation, each experience had built upon the last, leading to these ambitious new endeavors. With a firm resolve and a clear vision for the future, he was ready to embark on this next phase of the foundation's journey, poised to bring archaeology into a new era of global engagement and discovery.

As the year wound down, Nathanial Dove and Dr. Helen Carter took a moment to reflect on their personal growth and the evolution of their perspectives over the course of their recent endeavors with the Dove Foundation. They met in Nathanial's office, where the early evening light filtered through the windows, casting a soft glow over the room filled with artifacts and books—a testament to their life's work.

Nathanial, looking contemplative, turned to Dr. Carter. "Helen, when I think about where we started and where we are now, it's almost surreal. This foundation, our projects, they've grown beyond what I initially imagined. It's not just about the work, though. I've felt a profound shift in how I view our role as educators and stewards of history."

Dr. Carter smiled, acknowledging his sentiment. "I feel the same, Nathanial. It's been a journey of not just professional but personal growth. We've been pushed out of our academic comfort zones and into roles where we can genuinely make a difference. It's been challenging but incredibly rewarding."

Nathanial nodded. "Absolutely. And one of the things that have struck me most profoundly is the realization of how much more impactful our work can be when we actively involve the communities around these archaeological sites. It's changed my perspective on what it means to be an archaeologist in the modern world."

Dr. Carter leaned back in her chair, thoughtful. "Yes, the community involvement aspect has been enlightening. It's one thing to uncover history; it's another to help people connect with it, to see it as a part of their identity. That's where real change happens."

"The Global Heritage Initiative is going to be a significant step in that direction," Nathanial added, his voice filled with anticipation. "Bringing those communities into the conversation from the start, making them active participants rather than just observers."

Dr. Carter agreed, "It's about empowerment, isn't it? Empowering people to not only appreciate their heritage but to protect and celebrate it. And through the Virtual Archaeology Network, we can share that empowerment globally, which is just as exciting."

Nathanial chuckled slightly. "When I started my career, I never imagined I'd be talking about global networks or virtual reality. I was focused on the dirt, the artifacts. Now, I see those things as tools to connect people, to educate and inspire."

"That's a significant shift," Dr. Carter observed. "And speaking of shifts, I've noticed how much more collaborative our work has become. We're not just working within our team but with experts and communities worldwide. It feels like we're building something much bigger than any one of us."

Nathanial smiled, his eyes reflecting a mix of pride and humility. "That's the dream, isn't it? To build something that lasts, that makes a difference. I think we're on the right path."

As they prepared to leave the office, Nathanial stopped by the window, looking out at the quiet campus below. "Helen, thank you for being part of this journey. Your insights and leadership have been invaluable. I'm looking forward to seeing where we go from here."

Dr. Carter joined him at the window, sharing the view. "Thank you, Nathanial. It's been an incredible journey, and like you, I'm excited about the future. Let's keep pushing the boundaries, exploring new ideas, and making history accessible to everyone."

They left the office together, the conversations about the past mingling with plans for the future, a testament to their shared commitment to growth, learning, and making a lasting impact through their work. As the foundation moved forward, they carried with them a renewed sense of purpose, driven by the knowledge that their efforts were part of a larger, global narrative of connection and discovery.

Chapter 20
A New Dawn

In the brightly lit main hall of the Dove Foundation, festoons and banners hung from the ceiling, each adorned with images of ancient artifacts and digital renderings of archaeological sites. The occasion was the foundation's first anniversary, a milestone that marked a year of significant achievements and groundbreaking initiatives. Nathanial Dove and Dr. Helen Carter were busy greeting guests—scholars, educators, philanthropists, and students who had contributed to or benefited from the foundation's projects.

As the room filled with the hum of excited conversations, Nathanial stepped up to the podium to address the gathering. "Good evening, everyone. It's heartening to see so many familiar faces and new ones here tonight. This celebration is not just about the Dove Foundation's achievements, but about all of you, the community that has made this work possible."

Dr. Carter joined him, her voice carrying warmly over the crowd. "This past year has been a journey of discovery, learning, and connection. Thanks to your support, we've launched educational programs that have reached over a thousand classrooms globally, and our Virtual Archaeology Network is fostering a new appreciation for cultural heritage."

Nathanial nodded, his eyes scanning the crowd. "We've seen our initiatives bring history to life for students in ways that textbooks never could. Our interactive digs and virtual reality tours have allowed students from all over the world to 'touch' history."

A guest from the audience, a professor who had collaborated with the foundation, stood up to speak. "Nathanial, Helen, your work is transforming how we teach history and archaeology. The resources you've provided have enriched my lectures and seminars immensely. The interactive platforms are particularly popular among my students."

Dr. Carter smiled at the feedback. "Thank you, Professor. It's feedback like yours that drives us to keep improving and expanding our reach. We are particularly excited about our upcoming projects that build on what we've learned this past year."

Nathanial continued, "Indeed, Helen. And tonight, we also want to give a special thanks to our technology team, led by Marcus, who couldn't be here tonight. They've worked tirelessly to ensure that our digital platforms are not only educational but also accessible."

The mention of the tech team prompted applause, and a young attendee asked, "Could you share more about what's next for the Dove Foundation? What can we look forward to in the coming year?"

Nathanial responded with enthusiasm, "We are planning to launch a new series of field projects that will not only involve digging but also a comprehensive community engagement strategy to ensure that the local populations are active participants in the excavations and the preservation of their heritage."

Dr. Carter added, "And on the educational front, we're developing a new curriculum that integrates augmented reality more deeply, allowing students to experience historical events and daily life in ancient civilizations as if they were there."

As the presentations concluded, the floor was opened for mingling and celebration. Nathanial and Dr. Carter made their rounds, speaking with guests, exchanging ideas, and discussing potential collaborations. The atmosphere was vibrant, filled with a sense of accomplishment and anticipation for the future.

In a quieter moment, Nathanial and Dr. Carter reflected on the evening. "It's amazing to see how much we've accomplished in just one year," Nathanial remarked, a note of pride in his voice.

Dr. Carter agreed, "Yes, and tonight's turnout is a testament to the impact of our work. It's incredible to think about how many lives we're touching, not just through education but through fostering a deeper connection to our global heritage."

As the evening drew to a close, the foundation's achievements were clear, not just in the projects completed or the technology developed, but in the community and relationships built. This network of passionate individuals and organizations was perhaps the most significant accomplishment of all, promising a bright future for the Dove Foundation and its mission to bridge past and present through education and technology.

In the wake of the first anniversary celebrations of the Dove Foundation, Nathanial Dove and Dr. Helen Carter gathered with their core team to discuss the expansion of their initiatives. The meeting, held in the foundation's spacious strategy room, was buzzing with ideas and the energy of potential new projects that promised to push their mission further into new territories and disciplines.

Nathanial opened the meeting with an overview of the strategic goals. "We've had a phenomenal start, but it's crucial that we keep the momentum going. Expanding our horizons not only geographically but also in our interdisciplinary approaches is key. Helen, could you start by updating us on the educational programs?"

Dr. Carter was prepared, her laptop open to a presentation. "Certainly, Nathanial. Based on the success of our existing programs, we're proposing to launch two major initiatives. First, we're looking to establish partnerships with educational institutions in Africa and Southeast Asia. These regions have rich histories that are often underrepresented in global archaeological discourse."

"That's a fantastic direction," Nathanial responded enthusiastically. "What kind of support do we anticipate needing from local partners?"

"We'll need local educators and archaeologists on board to ensure that the programs are not only relevant but also culturally sensitive," Dr. Carter explained. "I propose a series of exploratory workshops with potential partners in each region to understand their needs and expectations."

Marcus, joining the discussion via video call, added his perspective regarding the technological needs. "For these new regions, we might face additional challenges, particularly in terms of technological infrastructure. However, this also presents an opportunity to innovate with low-bandwidth solutions for our VR and AR applications."

"That's an excellent point, Marcus," Nathanial acknowledged. "Let's allocate resources to research and develop these technologies. Making our programs accessible despite technological barriers is crucial."

The conversation shifted to another significant proposal on the table. Dr. Carter continued, "The second initiative involves developing a cross-disciplinary program that integrates environmental science with archaeology. Given the impact of climate change on archaeological sites, this program would not only educate but also engage students in active preservation efforts."

Nathanial was visibly excited by this idea. "That's groundbreaking, Helen. It aligns perfectly with our mission of education and preservation. How do you envision the structure of this program?"

Dr. Carter outlined her vision. "It would be a collaborative curriculum involving environmental scientists and archaeologists. We would develop case studies that show the impact of environmental changes on archaeological sites and explore how sustainable practices can be employed to protect these treasures."

"I see a lot of potential for grants and environmental partnerships with this initiative," Nathanial noted. "Let's draft a detailed proposal. I think it could attract significant interest from both educational and environmental organizations."

As the meeting drew to a close, the team discussed timelines and responsibilities for the proposed initiatives. Nathanial concluded, "These projects represent ambitious expansions of our work. They will require dedication and creativity, but I am confident that with our combined efforts, we can make them successful."

The team left the meeting energized, ready to tackle the challenges of expanding their reach and impact. Dr. Carter stayed behind to speak with Nathanial. "These are exciting times, Nathanial. It feels like we're not just part of history, but actively shaping it."

Nathanial smiled in agreement. "Indeed, Helen. It's about more than discovering the past; it's about ensuring that the past continues to inform and enrich the future. Let's keep pushing the boundaries."

With new projects on the horizon and a clear vision for the future, the Dove Foundation was poised to enter a new phase of growth, one that promised to further their impact on education, preservation, and the global understanding of cultural heritage.

In a quieter moment amidst the flurry of planning and expansion, Nathanial Dove took the opportunity to reflect on his own personal milestones alongside Dr. Helen Carter, as they shared a late afternoon coffee in the small café across from the Dove Foundation's headquarters. The café, with its walls lined with historical artifacts and photos from various digs, provided a fitting backdrop for their conversation.

Nathanial started, his tone contemplative. "Helen, when I think about the past few years, it's not just the foundation's achievements that stand out. It's also the personal milestones we've reached. It's been quite a journey, hasn't it?"

Dr. Carter smiled, stirring her coffee. "It really has, Nathanial. Starting this foundation was a leap into the unknown. Personally, it's been more rewarding than I could have imagined. Watching our projects take shape and actually impact people's lives—there's a real sense of fulfillment in that."

Nathanial nodded, his gaze reflecting a mix of pride and nostalgia. "For me, one of the most significant milestones was seeing our Virtual Archaeology Network go live. That was a dream for so long, and to see it actually functioning, connecting people across the globe to our work—it's incredible."

Dr. Carter agreed, "Absolutely, and for me, developing the educational programs, especially those for kids in underserved regions, has been profoundly rewarding. Knowing that we're opening up new worlds to them, it's a reminder of why we started all of this."

The conversation turned to the challenges they had faced. "There were moments I doubted we could pull this off," Nathanial admitted. "The logistical and financial hurdles, not to mention the occasional bureaucratic nightmare. But overcoming those challenges, it's taught me resilience, and a lot about leadership."

Dr. Carter laughed lightly. "Oh, the challenges. Yes, they were daunting. But you're right, overcoming them was an education in itself. For me, it was learning to negotiate and collaborate effectively, especially with people who might not share our vision. It's about finding common ground and keeping the bigger picture in focus."

Nathanial took a sip of his coffee, his mind seemingly sifting through memories. "Helen, when you think about the future, what are some of the milestones you're hoping to achieve, personally?"

Dr. Carter thought for a moment. "I'd like to see our educational outreach become a model for others, not just in archaeology but in all fields of science and humanities. Personally, I'd like to write more, perhaps a book about the role of archaeology in contemporary education."

"That sounds wonderful, Helen. As for me, I hope to continue growing as a leader, to steer this foundation into new territories, literally and figuratively. I'd also like to get back into the field more often, to reconnect with the roots of our work."

As they finished their coffees, both felt a renewed sense of purpose and excitement for the future. They stood up, ready to head back to the office, each buoyed by the other's aspirations and commitment.

Dr. Carter put on her coat, turning to Nathanial. "These conversations are important, Nathanial. They remind us of why we do what we do, and they reinvigorate our passion. Let's make sure to keep setting personal milestones too. They're just as important as our professional ones."

Nathanial agreed wholeheartedly. "Absolutely, Helen. It's those personal milestones that keep us grounded and drive us forward. Here's to many more for both of us."

With that, they stepped out of the café, back into the brisk air, ready to tackle the next challenges and opportunities that awaited them, both for the foundation and for themselves personally. As they walked, their conversation shifted back to the tasks at hand, but the underlying current of personal growth and renewal remained, a quiet yet powerful force driving them onward.

As the year drew to a close, Nathanial Dove took a moment to stand alone on the balcony of the Dove Foundation's headquarters, overlooking the expansive grounds that had become a symbol of the foundation's growth and impact. The winter air was crisp, and the sky was a clear blue, mirroring his thoughts about the foundation's future.

Inside his office, Nathanial had maps and charts spread across his desk, each representing different parts of the world where the Dove Foundation had made its mark and others where he hoped to extend its reach. The recent discussions and feedback sessions had given him much to think about, and now, it was time to chart the course forward.

Nathanial's thoughts were interrupted by a gentle knock on the door. Dr. Helen Carter entered, her presence always a sign of partnership and progress. She carried with her a digital tablet, her expression one of determined optimism.

"Nathanial, I've been reviewing our projections and feedback from the last quarter. It looks like we're ready to move forward with the new initiatives we discussed," she said, handing him the tablet.

Nathanial took it, scanning the information quickly. "Thanks, Helen. It's reassuring to see that the groundwork we've laid is solid. These new projects, especially the Global Heritage Initiative, are going to take a lot of resources, but I believe they're the right steps forward."

Dr. Carter nodded, her gaze following his to the window overlooking the gardens below. "I agree. And with our growing team and the new partnerships we've established, I think we're well-prepared for the challenges ahead."

Nathanial placed the tablet down, folding his hands thoughtfully. "We've built something truly remarkable here, Helen. But it's the next few years that will really define the legacy of the Dove Foundation. We're not just creating a network; we're fostering a global community that values and preserves history."

"Yes, and it's about more than preservation," Dr. Carter added. "It's about making history accessible and relevant to new generations. Our work helps people see the value of the past in their modern lives."

Nathanial smiled, the weight of their responsibilities clear but not unwelcome. "Exactly. And as we expand, we must continue to innovate not only in how we conduct our projects but also in how we engage with the public and our educational audiences. It's about keeping the human connection at the forefront of what we do."

As Dr. Carter prepared to leave the office, she turned back briefly. "Nathanial, I just want to say—it's been an incredible journey so far. Here's to the future and all it holds."

"Here's to the future," Nathanial echoed, his voice firm with resolve.

After Dr. Carter left, Nathanial returned to his balcony, looking out over the landscape. The setting sun cast long shadows across the grounds, a reminder of the passage of time and the urgency of their work. He thought about the new archaeological sites they planned to explore and the educational programs that would bring these discoveries to life for people around the world.

The challenges were daunting, but Nathanial was undeterred. He knew that each step forward was a step toward enlightening the world about the importance of history. The Dove Foundation had become a beacon of knowledge and innovation, and as the sun dipped below the horizon, Nathanial felt a profound sense of anticipation for what the future might bring.

With a final glance at the peaceful evening, he turned back inside, ready to tackle the necessary preparations for the coming year. The future was bright, filled with potential, and Nathanial was ready to lead the foundation into the new dawn.

In the calm of his office surrounded by the artifacts that told countless stories of civilizations long gone, Nathanial Dove found himself in a deep conversation with Dr. Helen Carter about the legacy they hoped to build through the Dove Foundation. As the late afternoon sunlight filtered through the windows, their dialogue touched upon the profound impact of their work.

"Helen, as we look forward to expanding our initiatives, I've been thinking a lot about the kind of legacy we're building," Nathanial began, his tone reflective. "It's not just about the discoveries we make, but about the knowledge we pass on."

Dr. Carter nodded thoughtfully, her eyes bright with the passion that had driven her work for years. "Absolutely, Nathanial. It's about creating a legacy of learning. We want to ignite a curiosity about the past that will endure, inspiring future generations to continue exploring and preserving history."

Nathanial leaned forward, his hands clasped together on the desk. "That's precisely it. And I think our educational programs are at the heart of this legacy. They're not just teaching facts; they're teaching critical thinking and respect for the past."

Dr. Carter smiled, clearly in agreement. "And the beauty of it is seeing how young people react when they realize history is not static. It's dynamic and it's relevant. Our work helps them see that they are a part of history, not just passive observers."

Nathanial picked up a small artifact from his desk, a pottery shard from an ancient Mesopotamian site, turning it over in his hands. "Each of these pieces tells a story, and each story is a lesson. Our job is to make these lessons accessible and engaging."

Dr. Carter watched him, her mind seemingly projecting into the future. "Imagine a world where every young person learns to appreciate the intricacies of history and its impact on the present. That's the world we're helping to create."

Nathanial set the shard down gently. "It's a powerful vision, Helen. And it's becoming a reality thanks to the dedication of our entire team. But as we grow, how do we ensure that this vision remains clear? How do we stay true to our mission?"

"That's the challenge," Dr. Carter acknowledged. "We must be vigilant, always ensuring that our growth enhances our mission rather than diluting it. Regular reviews, feedback sessions like the ones we've been conducting, and staying connected to the educational community are all crucial."

Nathanial nodded. "Right. And perhaps more importantly, we need to keep documenting our journey. Not just the successes, but the challenges too. Let's be transparent about what works and what doesn't."

Dr. Carter stood up, ready to leave but paused at the door. "Nathanial, working on this with you, seeing the impact we've made—it's been one of the greatest experiences of my professional life. I truly believe we are building something that will last."

Nathanial looked up, a genuine smile crossing his features. "Thank you, Helen. I couldn't ask for a better partner in this endeavor. Here's to many more years of making history together."

As Dr. Carter left, Nathanial turned his gaze out the window, watching as the sun began to set, casting a golden glow across the sky. The day was ending, but their work was far from done. Each day brought new opportunities to learn and teach, to explore and preserve. The legacy of the Dove Foundation was indeed one of learning, and as night fell, Nathanial felt a renewed sense of purpose and optimism for the future. This was just the beginning, and the path ahead was rich with potential.

Conclusion

As the sun set on another year at the Dove Foundation, Nathanial Dove stood once again on the balcony of the foundation's headquarters, reflecting on the journey that had unfolded. The foundation had grown from a mere concept into a thriving beacon of education and preservation, touching the lives of countless individuals across the globe. Under his leadership, and with the indispensable partnership of Dr. Helen Carter, the foundation had set a new standard for how archaeology could be appreciated and understood in the modern world.

The challenges had been many, from technological hurdles to logistical dilemmas, but each challenge had been met with determination and innovative thinking. The Virtual Archaeology Network was now a hub of global education, bringing ancient civilizations to life for students in remote corners of the world. The Global Heritage Initiative had transformed archaeological sites into centers of community development and cultural pride, ensuring that the benefits of preservation and research were shared with those who lived in the shadows of these ancient monuments.

But more than the projects and the technology, it was the people who stood at the heart of the foundation's success. Educators, students, archaeologists, and community leaders—people from all walks of life had come together to learn from and with each other. The foundation had sparked a dialogue about the past, one that was inclusive, respectful, and endlessly curious.

Nathanial knew that the road ahead would be filled with more challenges, but also more opportunities. As he looked out over the grounds, now quiet in the twilight, he felt a deep sense of fulfillment and anticipation. The Dove Foundation had not only discovered relics of the past; it had built a bridge to the future, one that promised to continue expanding the horizons of knowledge and understanding.

The story of the Dove Foundation was one of passion for the past and hope for the future, a testament to the enduring power of learning. It was a narrative that Nathanial and Dr. Carter, along with their ever-growing team, would continue to write in the years to come. Each artifact, each site, each student who discovered a love for history was a part of this legacy—a legacy not just of discovering history, but of making it.

As the stars began to appear in the evening sky, Nathanial turned from the balcony to go inside, ready to plan for the next day, the next project, the next discovery. The journey was far from over, and the next chapter promised to be as enriching as the last. With a renewed spirit, he stepped forward, ready to continue the foundation's mission to enlighten, educate, and inspire. The legacy of learning was alive and thriving, echoing through the ages, a beacon of light guiding the way to understanding the past and shaping the future.

www.ingramcontent.com/pod-product-compliance
Lightning Source LLC
Chambersburg PA
CBHW021957120726
47992CB00001B/295